A Short Joy for Alma Hedman

A Short Joy for Alma Hedman

By
Frances Webb

Strategic Book Publishing and Rights Co.

Strategic Book Publishing & Rights Co., LLC
USA | Singapore
www.sbpra.com

For information about special discounts for bulk purchases, please contact Strategic Book Publishing and Rights Co. Special Sales, at bookorder@sbpra.net.

ISBN: 978-1-946539-99-1

To

David and to all the ESL students in my life

Acknowledgments

Novels don't happen out of whole cloth. They happen because countless supportive people put time and effort into getting it between covers. This one owes its life to an imaginary rendering of many lives living in a large and extremely diverse city. I thank these many lives—all of whom and none of whom live in this novel—for making themselves available to me.

Thanks also to those who helped in this rendering—the readers, the critics, the typists, the hand holders, encouragers, the editors, the translators and the family—David for patient support, Aerie for her critical eye, sacrificial content and line editing, Tara, Deena and Andra for being there and Holly for organizing, formatting, and typing draft after draft. I thank Lyla and Terry for help with the Spanish and Terry for keeping me straight on the Spanglish and to Shari for keeping me organized. I thank colleagues and friends who patiently supported my efforts and were indispensable for the end result: Natalie Joy, Don, Quincy, Bette, Diana, whose written critiques have helped throughout, Linda, Rosemary, Elsa and many unnamed.

Special thanks go to Lillian and Jake, who were invaluable as astute readers, to Alice for her enthusiastic last-minute read and to Art for unblocking the periodic block.

I also want to thank the Sisters and staff of the Episcopal Silent Order Convent for providing a needed quiet retreat opportunity. Two books which were lovingly by my side, "The

Wisdom of the Saints" by Jill Haak Adels and "Lives of the Saints" by The Rev. Alban Butler deserve a special mention since they aided in the creation of the title character. Two books, which helped considerably in making the references to aspects of Santeria authentic and also occupied that aforementioned spot by my side, are "Santeria; African Magic in Latin America" by Migene Gonzalez-Wippler and "Rituals and Spells of Santeria" by Migene Gonzalez-Wippler.

I thank all bilingual schools of all levels for existing and especially the students who attend them, and I honor their commitment and their sacrifice in order to become more solidly useful members of their new country.

In addition, I acknowledge that Chapter 16, originally a short story entitled "A Piece of Paper with a Name on it", was published in SOUTH ROAD, Literary Journal of Martha's Vineyard, MA, Vol. 1, No. 2, in 1999.

Preface

Clunk!

"Stop it, Alma. Leave the kneeler up. We aren't praying yet."

Clunk!

"All right. Now leave it down. Just leave it *alone*."

"It does it itself."

"No, it doesn't."

Father John stepped away from the pulpit. His robe clung to his knees. It outlined his legs. Then his thighs. Clung to them.

Clunk!

"*Alma!*"

Alma pointed to the priest's legs. "Is that called static electricity?"

Mother winced.

Clunk!

She winced again.

Father John said, "Let us pray. May the words of my mouth and the meditation of my heart be acceptable to thee in thy sight, oh Lord." He leaned over and pulled his robe away from his legs. He straightened up.

The robe grabbed him again as he stepped behind the pulpit. "To continue our study of the origin of our church . . ."

Clunk!

"The Protestant Episcopal Church is derived from the Church of England . . ."

Clunk!
"Stop it, I said, Alma."
"…which was derived from the ancient British church, which already had a doctrine, a worship system, a diocese, sacraments, rites, and no doubt its saints …"
"Saint Bridgid's eyes split open and melted in her head."
"Alma, stop whispering!"
Clunk!
"*Shhhhhhhh.*"
"So, Pope Gregory was foiled. He couldn't establish the Catholic Church, and Augustine and his forty monks could do nothing in Britain, but he demanded submission to the Pope anyway."
Clunk!
"That's Saint Cecelia's head landing on the bathroom floor."
"I said, stop the whispering and sit up and listen to the sermon." Mother put her head in her hands.
Clunk!

***

"That's what you get, Agnes, for taking a seven-year-old to church."
"It's that confounded book you gave her, Muriel."
"How did I know? It's about saints—that can't be anything to worry about. I almost bought something called *Some Authentic Acts of the Early Martyrs*. It was reduced, on the remainder pile, but I thought that might be a bit too much for a seven-year-old to handle. You know, martyrs and all—they can be pretty rough on themselves, all those stigmata and such."
"Lots of saints were martyrs, so why you were so safe I don't know."

"She's filling her head with them. It's Saint Teresa this and Saint Clare that and Saint Agnes. She'll turn into a saint herself."

"Alma? A saint? She can't even chew with her mouth closed. She picks her nose and sasses her mother."

"I don't mean a saint that way. I mean, she'll try to emulate, or—"

"What's so bad about emulating saints?"

"Nothing, if she sticks to the good parts . . . you know, the holy parts. The other day she took a chair outside. I said, 'Where are you going with that chair?' 'To the moat,' she said. 'Why?' I asked. 'It's Saint Theresa's chair,' she said. I asked her why she needed a chair in the moat—wherever or whatever that was—and she said to sit on and pray and to listen to Saint Teresa say 'Come, come.' Are we going to let her go on like this?" "What can I do? I'm only her aunt. Shall I take the book back?"

"She'd have a fit. And it's probably too late anyway. She says the kitchen is Saint Catherine's, the music room is Saint Cecilia's, the parlor belongs to Saint Agatha, and each day is somebody's feast. She sits down for breakfast and says, 'Blessed be this food to thee,' dear Saint whomever, 'intercede this day of your birth and on behalf of all of those blessed ones,' and on and on she goes."

Chapter 1

Alma Hedman dropped her keys on St. Beggia's toes. She winced at the slapping sound and at the thought of Sister's last words to her, "Have no intercourse with the people in the world. Because, little by little, you will get a taste for their habits. Jean Baptiste de la Salle said that, Alma. Take heed, dear."

The door, heavy as always, opened enough for her to slide through and step outside. *For the wisdom of this world is foolishness with God.* "That," she said in a whisper into the afternoon stillness, "will have to be proven wrong."

A cool breeze swept across her legs as the door swung closed behind her. She walked down the sidewalk to the end, and then moved to the grassy area by the curb. Except it wasn't grassy today—it was muddy, and the earth was softening more from this drizzle. In fact, it was turning to mud, and she was going to leave a footprint of mud in Mama's car and a coating of it on the floor. *Mama will not be happy. If she ever gets here.*

But the words she was hearing now had nothing to do with mud. "Alma, you never finish anything you start. First this college, then that college, then a convent, and then not a convent."

Come on, Mother, this mud is going to dry and cake into hard-packed earth. The sisters will come out, and goodbyes will have to be said all over again, even if lovingly. They did say them so lovingly, so liturgically. "The saints fell in Adam, as we do. Remember, we sinners are also Christ working in the world. You will work in the world, dear Alma." Not "Sister Alma Margaret" anymore, but "Dear Alma," as she had folded her habit and put it in the chest from where it had come and laid the cross on top, careful to keep Sister Margaret's napkin ring from falling from her finger into the chest.

"Keep the napkin ring, dear. Let it be a talisman," she said as it spun around her finger.

Walking into the vestibule that first day, she had felt the sculpted saint staring at her. The inner door behind her had opened, and a soft voice had lovingly said, "I thought I felt a presence here."

"I'm here because—"

"Step in."

"I'm here to—"

"Yes, step in."

"The reason I'm here is—"

"I know why you're here. I just need to know your name. Come this way and tell me your name."

"Alma Hedman."

"Lovely, lovely. I can cross your name off now that you have arrived. Here are your keys, dear. We've solved the problem of lost keys. Every postulant has a spot on Saint Beggia here in the vestibule. Her hand, her foot, her knee, what part of her would you like, dear? Her hand, her foot, her knee, her what? Her toes? Yes, why don't you take her toes? So when you come in after your day's activities, whatever they turn out to be, and of course they are the ones you will leave us for every day, you drop your keys on her toes. That way you will always know where they are, and I and Mother Superior will be free of the postulant cry, as we call it, the 'where are my keys' cry. I'm sure you understand."

Yes, she had understood. And now she was leaving.

One year and two months of silence. Glorious silence. Except of course when in the classroom.

"Don't go, Sister."

"I love you all, and remember the words of the saint. 'Perfection does not consist of not seeing the world, but in not having a taste or relish for it.' And remember the mood of the verb in the subjunctive. Remember the difference of mood between the imperative, indicative, and the subjunctive. 'If this be the case'—"

"Don't go, Sister."

She caught the napkin ring at the edge of her finger, took it off, and put it in her pocket. With the mud hardened, there would be no footprint. Words of a saint floated in her mind, along with the clouds floating in the sky: *All the ways of the world are as fickle and unstable as a sudden storm at sea. And If I could live in a tiny dwelling on a rock in the ocean, surrounded by swelling waves . . .*

But she was entering the world now, so she'd better forget about that tiny dwelling. She just needed to remember what Sister had said, that "as long as we have peace with the natures of the world, we are enemies of God and of His angels and of all His saints." Then she had said, "Those are the words of Saint . . ." somebody or other. She couldn't remember who, but no matter that, "Just remember to keep your distance from the world's evils," she had said.

Dark clouds were floating up from the horizon. Luckily, she had her umbrella. *So, Mother better get here before they let loose with rain.*

Chapter 2

A car pulled up to the curb and stopped. The window on the passenger side rolled down.

"Be sure you step over that mud when you get in, Alma."

"It's not mud anymore, Mama, it's hard dirt."

"Are you saying I took too long getting here? I'm sorry. Bad traffic. And where am I supposed to take you? Are you coming home? You never finish anything. Once we got used to this nun business, we thought you were settled. We just want you to be happy."

"I was . . . I am . . . I was." Alma opened the door and slid onto the seat, putting her luggage between her legs.

"How can you be happy without a man?"

"I have something better."

"Hogwash. I've heard that before. It's crazy. It's a delusion. Just a fantasy."

"Virginity is the highest calling, Mama."

"Who said that? And how did this nut expect the world to continue?"

"It allows one to concentrate on the souls of the world."

"I just had an idea. You obviously have no clothes, let alone a house or anything that would go in one, or even a job. We'll stop at Bloomies on the way home and dress you and then get a bite to eat."

"All the ways of the world are as fickle and unstable as a sudden storm at sea." Alma knocked a piece of mud on her shoe onto the floor.

"If that's the case, what about all these souls you say you are going to concentrate on? Are they this job you are talking about that you don't have? And aren't they part of this fickle and unstable world? I assume it's a saint who said *that*. Are you going to quote saints to me? Can't you leave that back at the convent? Every letter I got from you was full of saints, and I don't want to hear them now. We will get a few skirts, some blouses. How are you for underwear?"

"That wasn't a saint. It was Bede the Venerable. 'If I could live in a tiny dwelling on a rock in the ocean, surrounded by swelling waves, cut off—'"

"That's enough."

"'May the Lord bless you and keep you and make his eyes to shine upon you—'"

"Stop it."

"That's only the benediction, not a saint. And besides, did you know that the love of worldly possessions is a sort of birdlime, which entangles the soul and prevents it flying to God?"

The car swerved.

Alma looked at her mother. The fire of demons was rising from the steering wheel. Her hands were white and clenched.

"The Lord neither broke bruised reed nor quenched smoking flax," Alma said, knocking mud off of the other shoe.

"Do you have to drip all that mud in the car? And no more saints, you hear? I drive all the way out here to get you, and you never say a word except to bombard me with saints. Did you do anything else in that convent besides talk to saints?"

"I taught in the school."

"Well, good. You did mention that. What did you teach? The saints?"

"No, the subjunctive."

"You said it was a silent order. We're coming to Bloomies. So, how did you manage to teach without talking?"

"We were silent at meals and other times . . . when—just other times, most of the time, almost all the time we were together. Except Sister said at our first dinner we could talk. She gave out napkin rings and napkins and said, 'They are yours. Remember the pattern.' Then she told a story about a singer in the choir and a cat that got on the piano. And 'By gomps,' she said, 'the cat looked down her throat just as she hit a high C and let out a piercing meow!'"

"That's a silly story. Why not talk all the time? Now you're probably all out of practice."

"I am. I'll try to talk. I'm still . . . it's hard."

"Crazy. Anyway, tell me about this convent, besides that it was silent."

"The convent was sweet. It was a sweet experience."

"Sweet? I never heard of 'sweet' for a convent."

"You know, hypnotic. 'Hail Mother, Mother of God,' over and over."

"So that's what you mean by sweet?"

"No. I don't know. I don't know what I mean. I'm just remembering."

"So, the nun thing didn't work out."

Her mother's hand on the steering wheel looked even whiter, and her words seemed spat out of her mouth. "Which saint was it that has set you on a different path, set you on leaving? Those damn saints got you into it in the first place, and now they're getting you out of it, right?"

"Okay, blame it on a saint if you want. How about Nicolas of Flue, Mother. He said, 'Each state of life has its special duties; by their accomplishments one may find happiness in the world as well as in solitude, for not all are called to separate themselves from the society of men."

"See? The society of *men*. Is that why you're leaving? For a man? If that's the reason, I approve."

"No. I got bored. And they changed the liturgy. Instead of thee and thou, it's you this and you that and—"

"Like I said, we're coming to Bloomies. Then home. The aunts are eager to see you."

Remember what Clement of Alexandria said, dear Alma, as you go into the world? "He, then, who faultlessly acts the drama of life which God has given him to play, knows both what is to be done and what is to be endured." And remember, pray in the society of angels. You are never out of their holy keeping. Would you like to keep your napkin ring?

"Good idea, Sister", Alma said to herself, and to her mother, she said, "I think I will not go home."

"What do you mean, not go home? I'm supposed to drop you off in the city? On the street? Just like that? What will the aunts say when I show up without you? And that hope chest I started for you . . ."

Do not be disturbed. "and, anyway, the linen can be turned into purification cloths."

"You talk gibberish."

"All the ways of the world are as fickle and—*stop the car, Mother!*"

The car swerved, scraped the curb, and stopped.

Alma opened the car door and got out. She stood on the sidewalk facing the car. She could see her mother's feet, one on the brake, the other flat on the floor. She could see the tip of her skirt just below her knees. "Goodbye," she said, bending to look into the car window to perhaps see her face also.

"That's enough, Alma. Stop this. You can't . . . I can't stop in this traffic. Get back in at once."

"No, I can't go home, Mother."

"I can't stop here."

"I know."

"What will you do? I have to move . . . these honks."

The car moved ahead and Alma heard through a muffled haze, "Go find a church then."

Alma leaned against the side of the Greater Appalachia Savings and Loan and watched her mother's car turn the corner and slowly join the traffic.

The cold brick of the bank building numbed her back.

Chapter 3

Carmelo had heard about snow.

He thought how everybody had said about snow, "You need boots."

He stood outside Kennedy Airport and watched for his brother. He watched the snow come down, a cold mistake from heaven. *¡Pero, muy bonita!*

He held out his hand and snow melted into the creases of his palm. His brother would come in a minute. In a black sedan.

"Watch," he had said, "because I no want to park, because it cost mucho, mucho money."

So many people! So many people from different countries. He could tell the Americans. Their white faces made them look sick. Mami said everybody up there was white. She said all the bosses were white. She said, "They won't want you, Carmelo."

His brother would come in a minute. His brother, with a wife and a job! He would get a wife and a job. Miguelina would come and be his wife.

If he waited long and Mario didn't come, he would get on the plane again, but a different plane—the one that got him here was no good. When it was leaving San Juan it got stuck on the ground and didn't leave for many hours. But he would get on one here if his brother didn't come, and go back to his country and get a coconut from the palm and open and drink the sweet water. If Mario did come, he would stay. He could, maybe, be a collision man, repair cars. He would do the body work. He would work on diesel motors. He was going to get rich from diesel motors. New York City was the city of the money.

"Carmelo, Carmelo, *mi hermano, pequito tito, Carmelito hermanito.* Hey bro, get in, get in. Put it there. *Vente, vente montate en mi caro.*"

Ah Mario! "Mario!" What did his brother expect? Of course he would get in his car.

Chapter 4

Carmelo looked at his brother through the car window. Different. He looked different. Older. Fatter.

"Get in. Get in! We gotta move from here. This here is no *parkiando*."

A policeman? Staring at his brother? Hand on his gun? A gun in America?

"I *said* get in. This here no park and no stand."

Wait. His luggage. "*Mi equipaje*," he said and threw his bag onto the backseat. Good. He got it before the policeman shot them.

"'Bout time. Didja see that cop? Put attention here, bro. But God you grew. Youse a long, lean man. But your smile, it the same big, wide, mean smile, man. I brought ya a coat."

Mario put his foot on the accelerator and the car jumped forward. "So tell me, hermanito, the trip, how was it? Smooth? Rough? Problemas? How is Mamita? Ya cold? In the back there, a coat, like I said."

"No problemas. *¿Pero por qué tu me hablas en Inglés siempre?*"

"Hey man, come on, get with it. You in the States now. English is the language, and that is the language I always speak to you in. 'Member that. And ya better speak it to me. Not like you don't know *none* a it."

He didn't think about that before he came. They speak Spanish, everybody said, in New York.

"Put attention to where you going, Carmelo baby. This you new city."

He was paying attention. Why did his brother have to talk to him in English?

"This here's the Triborough Bridge. You never saw so many bridges. We ain't got nothin' like them bridges in PR."

And nothing like the lights. Or so many cars, except maybe in San Juan. No, more here, and only a tiny bit of sky. "*¿Por qué tu me hablas in Inglés?*"

"I *said* because *this is America*. And the first thing you gotta do is get your ass into a school and learn you all that English what you don't have. Like you got some listenin' English, but no speakin' of it."

"No! *Primero el trabajo.*"

"No, first is no work. First is school, like I say. And see? Like I say, you knowed some English already. You understand me."

"*Comprendo, sí—tambien—el trabajo. La eascuela es para menores.*"

"It may be for babies, *pero* you no *es* a total grownup. And ya better *escucha* to your bro, Carmelito. Get a job later."

"*El trabajo ahora.*"

"No! Not now—after. And don't get no attitude. You gonna live with us, Maria and me. So you can get a job later. You'll like Maria. Una princesa. I got money. I got a little thing goin' that's good. Me and Rudolfo. Two things, but one I getting outta. And it be one you no get in. Just maybe someday the *otra* . . . maybe. I say you maybe help in that, okay? If not, okay. But get the English. Wanna burger? Wait 'til we get to Manhattan."

Carmelo looked out the window at this Manhattan that he was coming into so he could get a burger. Noise and dirt. Noise and bridges. Noise and tolls, his brother is calling them.

"This here is a toll. You pay here, hermanito, for everything—to go to a new bridge, to go to a tunnel, to go to a . . . Hey, you listenin' to me? It's English, so listen."

No silence from Mario. And what was he saying before? *A little thing goin'? Qué es 'a little thing goin'? ¿Y Quién es, Rudolfo?*

"Mira, mano. You learn that English. You know what happening to me yesterday? See your bro here? All the time these dudes swingin' at me sayin' 'Hey, bro, got a quarter?', 'cause they know, number one, I got it, and, number two, I'se them. One yesterday, he says, 'Hey, bro, you got any loose change? Like twenty-four quarters?' I look rich, man. That though is 'cause I wanna look rich, but that ain't real rich. It fake rich. It Rudolfo rich. That kinda rich ain't good rich. You? You gonna be *real* rich.

"Mira, mano, it's my talkin' bad that make me fake rich. If I be talking like them *pro*fessors, I be somethin' else. I be *real* rich. Because I talk a *hy*breed, and out there, hybreed don't make you make it. So that why I'm tellin' you, little bro, get yourself talking right from the beginnin'. You can, 'cause you ain't got no Rudolfos yet to learn you wrong. You hear me? *¡Vete a la escuela! ¡Por la Inglés!*"

Chapter 5

Alma walked through the church's narthex into the nave, turned so as not to face the altar, walked behind the end pews, turned again, and walked down the side aisle. She stopped at the transept. People were milling, getting ready for something, sitting.

She turned around and walked back. At the narthex again, she crossed to the nave, this time faced the altar, crossed herself, genuflected, and then continued to the other side aisle. She wandered down that one, looking here, looking there, considering this and that, until she came again to the transept. She stood then and watched the milling people—some children, medium-sized boys in white shirts and blue ties and blue pants, others, fathers maybe, mothers, aunts perhaps.

"Guest?" A young man put a paper, folded nicely, into her hand, and then motioned for her to sit.

She looked down at the paper. "The 24th Annual Confirmation Service and Graduation Ceremony of the Episcopal School for Special Boys." She thought for a moment to ask about one for special girls, ex-Episcopalian nuns, but instead shook her head toward the usher, telling him with unsaid words that she was not a guest, but a misplaced, or defrocked, sister and was looking for a . . . for a job? A home? Maybe a counselor, and not a graduation ceremony, as lovely as that sounded.

The usher again beckoned her to sit, and she smiled and shook her head again. "This way," he said. "I know we are a little late, but the boys will be processing soon, so do have a seat."

She sat. He left. She stood. A darkly robed father walked close and said, "And you are whose parent?"

"No one's. I have this," she fluttered the program, "because the usher gave it to me and I took it."

"You are welcome to join us."

"Thank you, but what I'd like is a . . . a . . . Do you suppose I could talk to a . . . to you maybe, or to a counselor? I just left the Novitiate of Saint Beggia in Basiltown."

"Excuse me. I did not know you were Sister . . . Sister who?"

"You don't know me, and I need some direction."

"Prayer, my dear."

"Yes, I know. But I need to talk to . . . to a person."

"For now, enjoy the boys. Later . . ." His voice trailed off, and Alma sat.

She listened to a recitation of names: Jose Cruz, Juan Hernandez, and on, and on. She watched the robed father hand over rolled-up, beribboned diplomas, and then she partook of the service, standing, kneeling, singing, praying, including communion, at which time she realized it was all in Spanish, and also that the wafer had been sticking to the roof of her mouth, and for the remainder of the service, including the final hymn and benediction, she tried to peel it off with her tongue, only to have it settle further into the vaulted recesses of the roof of her mouth.

Chapter 6

Money is what he wants, not English. If he gets a job and gets money, Miguelina can come here. Someday he'll be a collision man. Now, motors diesel. He knows them, motors, like he knows *plantons*. That's what he wants, *plantons*. Some sweet, sweet plantons. And what was that noise in Mario's engine?

"This thing I got goin', see . . ."

If his brother is going to talk English to him, he won't listen. He'll do something else with his head. He'll think about Miguelina. Feel her. Put his hands on her. Love, love her. Mmm.

"Hey, man, you ain't listenin' to me."

She likes the indentation in his chin. Kisses it. "*¿Dónde?*" she says.

"*Es papi's,*" he says. Papi. His no-good papi. Went to New York and was going to send money and he never did. He, Carmelo, will do that. He will send money to Mamita. She says he should be a priest. She says he'd be a good priest.

"Ya gonna listen to me, or ain't ya? I'm tellin' ya about this thing with Rudolfo, and you look like youse in dream world city! *¡Escucha, escucha!*"

Listen, listen! Listen to his brother? He would listen to himself. And there was something very wrong with his brother's engine.

"*¡Mira, mira!* This thing now, a little money on the side. Just know your market."

16

Mami says he'd be a good priest because he doesn't spend money. That's not it. He doesn't have money to spend.

"Be cool, be cool. Stay all the time on the top. That's the trouble with Rudolfo. He's on dope, at times anyways, and I'se the one that's gotta be in charge."

He almost missed the plane waiting in the cafeteria for her so she could bless him. Then she yells, "No eat pumpkin!", as if he didn't know not to eat pumpkin. As if he didn't know that would be bad luck. She knows he wants money. So why would he do that?

"He like his plays too much . . . *entonces*. He takes the money for the numbers . . . entonces. Gotta watch, and sometimes he get rough—that pot head part a him . . . tambien. Don't get me wrong. I gotta lotta likin' for Rudolfo, a lotta likin' for a gamblin' dope guy, 'cause he's got a little thing goin' wid me."

The airport was bad. Bad. Finding the telephone. Finding the luggage. And those three men at the luggage—PR men like him. Like always, he was high over them, so tall. And, like always, uncomfortable with that. Older—fathers, a grandfather—he could tell. And when the grandfather's box came on the beltway, it was broken, tied in blue ribbon by Eastern, a disaster.

They laughed at the disaster, and the younger one said to the grandfather, "You lost you chickens, Papi."

And the grandfather said, "No, I lose my turkey." The joke was too much for him, and he doubled himself over.

Why were they talking in English? To each other even? They didn't need to do that. He wasn't one of them anyway. He was too tall. He was too dark. And Mario better fix that *clunk clunk* before he loses his motor.

"You ain't listenin' again. ¡*Escucha, escucha, Y mano! Pero*, don't get me wrong. I like Rudolfo. He's made us all sing with money. Mira, Carmelo, down on that avenue . . ."

He is not going to stay. In two days he will go back. He can't even see the sky with all these bridges and buildings. His Puerto Rican sky is what he wants to see, the dome of it and the clouds of a thousand forms, black ones that let the rain out, and the white ones right beside that stop the rain. So close, the sky is so close, and not this snow.

"... down on that avenue, it's bad, man. It's bad. *Pero qué* ..."

And always his mountains, always there, beyond, but always there. And Miguelina, his love. "No, Carmelo," she had said, "don't go. Come back soon or I'll put a hex on you." She'd go to babalowa, she said, and ...

"Sure, I got a regular job. Did I tell ya? Yeah, I did, on the phone with Mamita. I'm an engineer. Head, boss, *el jefe*. I gives the orders. I told ya, remember? I say get the mop."

Look at fake, rich Mario behind the wheel of this big black sedan with the motor clunking. His brother, driving like Rambo and forgetting about his own mountains. Forgetting about being a little boy and being honest poor. "*¿Recuerde Guayabo?*"

"Yeah, sure I remember. Think I don't remember playin' baseball and swimming' and all that? So this Rudolfo, he ... See, there these places, man, where the clothes—designers' clothes—Cardin, Jordache, Klein Calvin. You name the jean, it's there. Come off the boat. China probably.

"Maria has this friend. She knows the dock people. The dock guys. And she has this deal going with them ... with us. Maria's my only love. Maria's beautiful. You'll see."

Chapter 7

"Yes, we do provide some counseling. I'll be in my office after the boys have received their final blessing and are on their way. It is through that door to the right of the narthex."

Alma nodded her thanks and sat back and watched the Father walk toward the altar, genuflect, turn toward the canopy of blue-jacketed boys, and raise his hands. She thought how she would no longer be blessed by Mother Superior. She let "May the Lord bless you and keep you" flow over her, and she heard in her head, underneath these soothing words, Aunt Tessie whispering to Mother in the back hall, "I almost bought *Some Authentic Acts of the Early Martyrs*. It was reduced, on the remainder pile."

What books did these boys get to read to want them to become what they were about to become? Were they reading about martyrs' eyes melting in their heads too?

***

"Have a seat, dear Sister Alma."

"Thank you, Father William, but I am no longer a nun."

"Yes, yes. I do understand that, but, in a sense, once a nun always a nun."

"I know. I was . . . am afraid of that. But, you see, I have . . . I need to move on. Saint Bridgid's eyes split open and melted in her head."

"What's that you said?"

"Nothing. Just, I have to move on. Get in the world a bit."

"Yes, that, but you said something about Saint Bridgid was it?"

"Hmm?"

"What is it about Saint Bridgid other than her martyrdom? Anything?"

"She vowed chastity, and her parents made her get married, so she asked for a deformity, and I thought that was pretty impressive."

"So even before puberty, you vowed chastity?"

"No, Saint Bridgid did."

"That could be a given for a nun, of course. You know—"

"Yes, but it wasn't that. It was that she fooled her parents. But right now, I need a job."

"Yes, yes, we'll get to that."

"She fooled the grownups."

"Yes, that can be enticing."

"But, like I said, right now I need a job, and I must enter the world. I believe it was Saint Nicholas of Flue who said—"

"Is that why you are here? I think you are here because you need help."

"I guess. But really—"

"Remember that as long as we have peace with the natures of this world, we are enemies of God and of His angels and of all His saints."

"Yes, I know, but—"

"What more do you remember about your early years?"

"I . . . don't know. And . . . and I need a place to stay . . . and a job."

"As I say, we will get to that. For now, let's continue our discussion of your interest in the saints. It is true that some of us travel that route. But we are all different, and we all hear the call differently. You seem to have heard it . . . umm . . . strangely. No matter how you hear the call, you can still do God's work now, in the world.

"And as for a place to stay, our church is so big you'd think we'd have a convent, but we do not. We do, though, rent rooms in the manse occasionally. And in exchange, do you think you'd like to work in our office? We need a soul there, goodness knows, now that Hilary Lapham has gone on maternity leave. I shall introduce you to Mrs. Roberts."

Chapter 8

Mario's Maria may be beautiful, but so is his Miguelina beautiful, and she should be here with him. She wants to be a singer. She tried at El Caribe, but they said to come back when she's older. Baby. They called her a baby. They said she was a baby. No, Miguelina is not a baby. A grownup. A grownup with a grownup body, and . . .

"So Maria, she gets the clothes out and Rudolfo has a truck, and he's there when she's coming out and hands them to Rudolfo and a friend, and quick-like, before you can say 'my name *es* Mario Rodriguez' they're in the truck, and Rudolfo—he's something man—is driving away and Maria is going to the subway and nobody is any different. The boss of his friend don't even miss 'em, and the guy to get the clothes to sell, he happy. He sell them on the street. Jeans. Piles of 'em. *Pero*, that all for later. Just 'member, here in this city you black. *You is black!* Don't get it into you head you is anything else. You, maybe, not so very, but you mi hermano, and look at me! Black, okay, but more brown. Rudolfo, he more brown than me, but one of us."

The snow on the windshield wasn't snow anymore now. It was rain. The way it ran down the glass was like lizards running for cover.

Chapter 9

"So, you were a teacher?" Mrs. Roberts put a cup of tea in front of Alma. "Sugar? Lemon? Milk?"

"Nothing, thank you."

"You'll want lemon, I'm sure." She dropped a piece of lemon on the saucer. Alma picked up her spoon and poked at the lemon pulp. The rind curled around the fruit like a bonnet.

"Our Hillary was good at reminding people to tithe. Father William is terrible at it. How do you think you'll be at that?"

"Excuse me?" She flipped the lemon wedge to the edge of the cup.

"Never mind. That's only one of our headaches."

"I'm used to headaches. I miss my students though." The lemon wedge teetered.

"You'll soon find a new life, my dear."

"Yes." She shoved it further onto the saucer.

"Could you tell me—this is just for my own curiosity—what is that that is surrounding your cross, which is surrounding your neck?"

"You mean this?" Alma lifted the napkin ring and put her finger through the hole. Her finger curled so as to enclose the tiny cross that nestled in its center.

"Yes."

"It was a gift. It was my napkin ring at the convent. I added the cross. Stuck it in sort of."

"That answers my curiosity. I just couldn't make out what it was. Thank you. I thought it looked like a napkin ring. Now I know for certain."

"Funny how we need to know, isn't it?"

"Yes, even merely the identification of an object."

The lemon, Alma noticed, had nestled beneath the cup and was oozing juice under it.

"Yes. Objects are mere trinkets of the devil, unless they represent the soul's ascension to the Lord," she said, studying the mini yellow flood.

"Well . . . yes, I guess you could put it that way."

Clunk! Saint Margaret turned into a dragon and then Satan swallowed her. *Clunk!* Saint Angela, the devil does not sleep, but seeks our ruin in a thousand ways. *Clunk!* Saint Clare, close your ears to the whisperings of hell and bravely oppose its onslaughts. *Clunk!*

"What is that you are mumbling under your breath?"

"Nothing, nothing. Did you know that the accounts of Saint Agnes have contradictions? I checked. One says she was stabbed in the throat and not the breast, and another says she was beheaded and not stabbed at all. And still another says she was rolled over coals naked, but I guess they could have done all of those things. None preclude the other. Wait, there is another version too, that her breasts were cut—"

"Umm, yes."

"I read this. In my saints' book."

"Is . . . um . . . Father William . . . I mean, tell me, is he doing some counseling with you?"

"He was, yes. Why?"

"I don't think . . . I mean, I believe . . . yes. I believe he intends to do more. I'll see. Yes, I'll see."

"I told him I needed two things, a job and a place to stay."

"Yes, we certainly have the latter."

"Thank you. That is a relief. I did not enjoy leaning on the side of the Appalachian Bank of New York. The bricks were mighty chilly."

Chapter 10

He was still bent from the plane. So long in it and so long on the seat that his back was aching. No, not so long, but long for him. And the plane couldn't make up its mind—keep going, go back, keep going, go back, engine trouble. So it went back and they started all over again in a new plane, and he watched all over again the mountains leave him and the sky change from its blue to a cloud big enough to cover El Moro.

"So learn English, bro. You gotta do more than just understand a word. Do you hear what I say, *muchochito*? I got English in my Spanish and Spanish in my English, and both of 'em in my talk, and that ain't good for jobs."

He knew English. But his own brother didn't need to talk to him in it. Even if he did know it, and he does know it. Got it from El Caribe, carrying luggage. "Where to?" "Room Fifteen." "Got it." And from school, when he studied anyway, before he left for diesel motor school. That sound he's hearing in Mario's big, black, fancy sedan is the transmission!

"*Mira*, Mario . . ."

"*¡Oh, mano!* Look at that over there, that piece. Mira, if you ain't fillin' it, you is chillin' it."

What woman was he talking about? Oh, that one leaning against that building. They were off the bridge now, so they were in Manhattan maybe? And that woman was a movie star maybe?

Carmelo opened the window and stuck his head out.

Mario slapped him in the face. "You *pavo pavo*."

"*No mi, Mario, tu.*" His brother was the turkey, not him. He wanted money, not women. First money, then Miguelina.

"*Entonces*, whatsamatter? You treatin' me with a attitude. You don't want a woman, okay. Don't go havin' a attitude about it with me. Did I tell ya I make a hundred a day sometimes, man? 'Specially the jewelry. God I forgot. I didn't tell ya about the jewelry."

Mario had the disease of the running mouth with a transmission about to fall out of his car.

"*Pero*, like I say, little bro, *escuela, escuela! ¡Tambien, no trabajo!*"

"*¡No escuela! ¡No escuela!*"

Chapter 11

Father William took his vestment off, tucked his shirt into the waist, fiddled with his belt, put his hands in and then out of his pockets, and sat down. "Tell me, Alma, just how old were you when you became so . . . so enamored of the saints and their lives, their stigmata and such?"

"I don't know, five maybe. But I'm not sure enamored is the word. It was . . . it was the book. I could read when I was three or four. Aunt Tess taught me. That PH has an *F* sound. Like E-fee-sians. Ephesians. 'Now read chapter two, verse two,' she said, and I did."

"I see. Another question, just why did you leave Saint Beggia's? You do not need to know that in order to do God's work now in the world, as you say, but it will help you to know. Our Lord is not a Lord of denial. He accepts you as you are and does not judge our . . . our . . . propensities, so to speak. Remember that."

"They changed the liturgy. By the way, thank you for allowing me to stay at the manse. Mrs. Roberts suggested that, and now I really need a job."

"Yes, yes . . . and I agree, the liturgy is different. But why did that make you want to leave?"

"I don't know. Everything became different then, when that happened. They changed the Canticles, they changed the Benedictus, they changed the Gloria and the Creed."

"Yes, I know."

"Instead of 'Lord have mercy upon us,' it's 'Lord in your mercy.' Instead of 'And with thy spirit,' it's 'And also with you,' and 'It is mete and right so to do' became 'It is right to give thanks and praise.' What was the matter with mete and right? What was wrong with that? Nothing was wrong. It's what I grew up with. And whatever happened to King James? And at Saint Beggia's all the 'thys' became 'yours,' and all the 'thous,' 'yous.' And 'Lord, hear our prayer' is 'Lord, open our lips.' 'Open our lips'? That's ridiculous. It's so anatomical. Anyhow, I'm off the subject, which is a job."

"I'm not sure you are ready, just yet, for a job, unless, as I mentioned before, we need someone in the office. However, that someone must be ... well ... someone who ... let's say—"

"I'm a teacher."

"Yes, yes, of course. That's what you should do. And I will see what I can do. It might take a while, however ... to—"

"Our labor here is brief, but the reward is eternal."

"You see, your mumbling like that could be a problem."

"If I could live in a tiny dwelling. Am I mumbling?"

Chapter 12

"You win, hermanito. Go get a job! You work and then you pay me rent, what I wasn't gonna take if you was in school. How's that?"

"*¡Sí, sí!*"

Mami said be good to your brother and he'll take care of you. She said you would need care because you are too sweet. Not like Mario, but Mario'll be good to you.

"*Pero*, when you gonna learn that English?"

"*¡No sé!*"

"Ya better know! *Pero*, you no got English, you needs lotsa luck."

Mamita said that about luck too, not to eat beans so he'd have luck. Not to eat pumpkins so he'd have money. And why was his big brother now slapping him on his back and picking a piece of paper out of the trash can? And writing on it? And handing it to him with crap on it from the garbage?

"Here, *tu loco!* And don't say 'took to the boss,' say 'talk to the boss.' Hear me? People will laugh if you says 'Can I took to the boss.'"

And why was Maria making pictures on a napkin and shoving him to the door?

"*¿Qué es*, Maria?"

"It's a train, dummy, and here's the street over the train, and it goes zoom zoom. It's what you gotta get on to look for a job.

And you go to the left out the door here. Derecho. The door to the subway is very big and wide and open to the sky, with stairs going down and down to where this train would zoom under the street. And the door on the train, they close fast. But first you come to a barrier, and you got to put this card through the slot," and she said more, but he didn't listen, because it was way too complicated.

"And this here is what I write and is what you say to people when you goes to the companies. Good luck!"

Mario opened the always-closed front door. "One block to the subway, and don't go losin' the paper which I *am* givin' to you, spite what I is thinking about it. You no got English, so you needs lotsa luck, like I say. Maybe this'll make you know you gotta have it, the English."

He picked up a box of clothes, lying in cellophane inside the box, that he was taking to where he was going to sell them to people who wanted them, he said, and wanted them at his prices, he said low, like a whisper, and stood holding the door, waiting— Carmelo could tell—until he went out the door first.

So he kissed Maria and walked through the door. It slammed behind him before he was completely over the sill, and the heel of his left foot skidded into the hall.

Okay, to the left. One block. There, that was it. Train tracks riding high across the avenue? Nothing like that in Barranquitas. She said the door was big and wide and open wide to the sky, a gaping door with no roof, just a black hole with stairs going down and down to where this train would zoom under the street before it vomited, she said, out of the tunnel and aimed for the heavens. How many flights? One. Two. Three. Now, on the platform, by the zooming train, and yes, it was doing that—zooming. But a barrier . . . yes, she did say . . . gave him a card, drew a picture, some little arrows pointing which way, and—

"Hey, dude, want some help?"

Carmelo looked around. A long arm came toward him, and with it some words. "Yeah, you, bud, you with the PR cap and yellow shirt, want some help? You a no-English-speaking Latin? Do you comprendo? You want some help with that card?"

Then the card went from his hand, fast like a lizard, and shot into the slot and out and back in his hand.

"Okay, go through! Go, go through. See, it says 'go' right there," and a finger pointed to a little green "Go."

He pushed himself against the turnstile and went through to where that train had zoooooomed. He turned and called "*gracias*," and that guardian angel yelled "de nada" and pushed his own magic card into the small magic slot.

Carmelo looked up and down the platform. Nobody but he, and now his guardian angel next to him. Somebody to take care of him. Somebody to watch over. In this new city. Just like that!

"Where you goin'?"

"*¿Habla Español?*" he said as an answer to a question he thought was "Dónde."

"*Sí. Un pequito.* Where ya goin', dude? *¿Dónde?*"

Ah! He speaks Spanish.

"Just got here? *Aquí. ¿Aquí? ¿Ahora?*"

"*Sí, sí.*"

"Here's the train. Be careful."

Yes, that awful noise. And he's got to think about the fast door.

"Whatsa matter? Why ya got your hands over your ears? Too loud for ya? I'm getting on here too. Come on. You gotta get on fast or you'll be a pancake in the door. You on? Okay, I gotta question for you? Got any money? Hey, I got a Blossom Bar on me, you know, candy bar. I'll let you have it for free—and it's worth a hell of a lot more than free—if you get off at the next stop and make a transaction. I got some dope in my back pocket besides this candy bar. Here, stick this in your pocket, and I betcha don't know a word I said. I said, '*Vette off con mio y* we make a deal. Just *vette off con mio.* It'll be *bueno para tu.*'"

Next stop? No, Mario said two stops for mechanic shops. This guy said "dope" and "money." No, better get away from him. He's bad. Bad. He'd go sit down between that old man and the grandmother.

He shook his head at his guardian angel who wasn't that at all, now he could tell, talking about drugs and all. He watched him make a fist and stick his finger up. And now the middle finger sticking up? "Fuck you too," he made his lips say.

Uh oh! He's coming over to him. Got his fists up.

"Okay, Bozo. Gimme that candy bar back."

He reached into his pocket, after he figured out what he was saying.

"*Quick!* Here comes a cop. Oh shit."

Good. He's moving to the other car. And he's still got the candy bar. Good. Nice. Nice snack if Maria's not cooking tonight.

He got off in two stops, like Mario said, and stood on the platform. Now what? Get out the crazy way he got in, but no place for the card. But people were getting out without it, so he could too. Follow them. Okay, follow them through that card-stealing gate, and go up those stairs over there.

He walked along the street looking at Mario's paper and remembering what he said. *Talk, talk, talk, not took.* "Not can I took to the boss," Mario said. He would practice.

He made his tongue do a different thing, and all the way on the street he said, "Talk, talk, can I talk to the boss?" and looked for the sign Mario said was here "Mechanic Wanted."

He walked inside the wide, gaping garage door and said to a back that was in front of him, "Can I took . . . talk to the boss?"

33

The back turned around. "Who's asking for the boss?"

"Yo, I." He slapped his chest.

"You wanna a job? I need a guy for phone work. How's your English?"

"*Bueno, bueno. Sé algunas palabras, una palabra por otra, una palabra aquí y aya . . .*" No, no, no. He shouldn't be talking in Spanish. Better try again, "*Bueno*, good. I know English. *Sé muchos palabras.* Mucho words."

"Hey, my customers are truckers, kid. They don't know no 'say una parabola' stuff." The boss went back behind a truck, and when the boss did not come back out from behind the truck, Carmelo knew the boss was saying "no," because he had said it in Spanish, and before that the boss was smiling.

He walked back through the gaping door and stood on the sidewalk. Mami said don't cry in public, so he pushed his fists into his eyes to keep that from happening. *No llores, no llores, no llores.* But he could not help it, and the tears welled.

He walked back down the street toward the subway, kicking his foot into the cracks of the sidewalk and slamming his fist onto the sides of cars parked like they owned the street, and stepped into the dark hole of the subway and walked down the stairs. He pulled his magic card—that was about as magic as a blade of grass—from his pocket and slid it through the slot, pushed the turnstile, and stepped onto the platform.

He was going back to PR. No, he had to stay, because he had said he was going to become a collision man back home, and they had said, "*¡Bueno!*", so he couldn't go back after he said he was going to be a collision man in the big city of the money and they had said "*¡Bueno!*"

The train rumbled in front of him and stopped. He waited while many, many people vomited from it. He stepped into the car. He sat. He stared at signs above the seats across from him through blurry eyes, signs that were in Spanish, signs for Soave Folonari and for places to get abortions it looked like. Maybe the Americans don't get abortions, and so they don't need a sign in English for that.

Rudolfo and the friend of Maria—what was her name? Renia? Renia was talking about that to Maria in front of Rudolfo, who was dating Renia, and that she was thinking maybe she was pregnant, and Maria was saying to her, "Get married," but Renia said, "No. I get the abortion."

Maria cried and said, "No, no. God give you that life," and Renia say, "That ain't no life, that a piece only of meat," and Rudolfo hit his fist on the table and the beer spilled.

Those signs are in Spanish, so why can't he talk to the bosses in Spanish? The Spanish is *there*. In public like that. Maybe he should work for Rudolfo. Rudolfo doesn't make him talk in English just because *he* talks in English all the time. But then Rudolfo buys crack, and he sells it, and he tells him not to tell Mario that.

"Hey, kid," he said that time, "maybe you don't want to get into the big crack business yet, but how about helping out with some pot dealing, and you can get a percent and you can forget about this truck body work business."

He steals clothes, too, and he sells them and he calls that his business. He *malo, malo, malo, a*nd he'll make *him malo malo malo!* If Rudolfo stood in front of him right now, he would hit him. *Bam!* Like that.

"Watch out. Watch what you doin', kid. Look at this crazy kook! Hittin' the air!"

"*Toma . . . hijo de la gran puta—maricon. Me cago en tu madre, toma.*" *Bam! Bam! Bam!* Ugh. His fist went into something soft.

"*¡Toma Rudolfo!*"

A thud sent him to the floor. His nose went into the subway floor, and when he took it out there was blood. All around him were sneakers and blood and yelling.

He is being pulled up. Making him stand. A policeman? He is looking at a policeman and the policeman is writing. And asking questions. In Spanish. So he can make his answers right, and all the time he is making his answers right he is thinking about his blue dome skies and Miguelina singing at El Carib.

Chapter 13

"I appreciate your help, Father William, and I have decided to accept your offer of working in your office."

"No, no, no. You are a teacher, and that is what you should do, and it just so happens that I have received some interesting information from my friends in high places. I am told that there's a new school, community college, part of the Great University, but more or less sort of an experiment, I believe, and not terribly fussy about whom they hire. I presume they would take anybody they can get, since it is in East Park, and seeing as who the students will be. But you can look at it as service, and I'm sure you would enjoy it, and . . . and I imagine they would take no notice of your propensity to mumble, but I might suggest that you try to curb that. And why don't you ask Mrs. Roberts to give you some pointers on clothing protocol for an interview? Ask for guidance. Ah, here is Mrs. Roberts."

He got up and walked toward the door, saying, "I leave you in good hands."

***

"That's better. I'm not sure you should wear the napkin ring. But if you insist, I won't dissuade you. Yes, the blue suit does bring out your eyes. Do you have the directions?"

"Yes."

"Out with you then. Go, go."

"I'm going."

"I'm closing the door. Goodbye."

Alma stood on the sidewalk. The traffic screeched by. Out of a silent world into another, only a noisy one and in another country. *Don't be disturbed by the drama of the world which passes like a shadow.* Okay, these rumbling roiling trucks and screeching taxis and rolling bobbing busses will pass like a shadow. She looked at the scribbled directions. They blurred.

Don't be disturbed. How could she not be? Yes, Sister had said, "Go and teach. You have been teaching. Don't let them think that teaching in a convent leaves a hole in your résumé. It's as real as the grace of God."

No, it's a hole on a piece of paper.

Chapter 14

"*¡Muchochito cojelo suavesito! ¡Muchochito cojelo suavesito!*"

Mario is looking at him. "Take it easy! Take it easy! I didn't bring your ass to New York City to fight some motherfucker in the subway."

Maria is putting her hand on his cheek and ice on his nose. "My poor baby! If you talk English this not happen. They no understand you and think you say something against them."

"No. No." He wasn't talking at all. He was just hitting into the air, but Maria and Mario and Rudolfo and Renia don't believe that he was only hitting into the air, hitting at nothing. They just keep saying "poor baby" and "take it easy, baby," like Mario kept saying first, and wouldn't believe him at all.

"I told ya! I told ya!" Mario's face is close to his. "Ya gotta talk English or they's gonna figure to put you in jail. It thaaaaaaaat simple. And what English you do talk, you motherfucker, you get the words all upside down. You gotta put the *right* word next to the *right* word, and if you ain't doing that, there ain't nobody what's gonna know what the hell this goddamn black motherfucker is saying, and they get par-E-noid, man, and think you is gonna fuck their mother and take their money or their woman or their fuckin' balls."

"*¿Por qué yo no trabajo, Mario?*"

"I told ya, ya *pavo estúpido, because you don't talk English!*"

"I no *need to took English to fit a motor diesel!*"

"Okay! You do talk some English. But you gotta talk more than that. Maria, you talk to him."

"Carmelo, baby." Maria's looking at him. Her eyes are going into his head. "It's truth. You no have to talk English to work a mechanic, *pero con todo* you still need it to *get* the job. So, go to school like you was going to in PR."

He couldn't stand her eyes piercing into his head like that. He moved her hand off his cheek and got up. He walked over to the telephone.

"You callin' Miguelina? You gonna go back? To see her? Or to go to school? Or what?"

"Nada."

He can't go home, but he *can* call Miguelina, and she will come. No, she won't come. She said for him to come back soon, real soon. What was soon? *¿Qué?* What's soon? And if he didn't do that, she would have his hairs pulled out, one by one by one.

He took his hand off the phone. Not get money that way, so why even call her?

"So what Miguelina say? She comin' *aquí?*"

"*Nada.*"

"Ha! So now maybe *escuela?* First school, then trabajo, then moolah, then Miguelina! That you schedule, bro!"

"No, Mario. *Trabajo, y munera, y Miguelina.*"

Chapter 15

Don't be disturbed.

She stood still and watched small sudden flakes of snow gather on her feet. She looked at the snow slowly covering them. She shook, first one and then the other, and walked toward the subway. She walked down the stairs to the subway platform. She swiped the metro card Father had given her and pushed through the turnstile and chalked the anxiety of that motion and the pleasure of it up to Saint Nicholas of Flue. "Each state of life has its special duties; by their accomplishments one may find happiness in the world as well as in solitude." She whispered this to herself over and over as she heard the rumble of a train coming toward her.

It stopped and the door opened. She stepped into the car, leaned on her umbrella, grabbed a bar, and held her body stiff as the train jerked, and then sped. "For not all are called to separate themselves from the society of men," she whispered to her strap-hanging arm. She had figured this philosophy out at the first silent meal after getting tiger looks from Sister Agnes when she asked for the salt, and then mentioned twice that there was a leak in the hall outside of the shower room.

At Sixteenth and The Boulevard, she stepped off onto the platform and fixed her face so as to assure the swarms of people that she knew exactly where she was, where she was going, and how to get there. She climbed the steps out of the subway.

Another country of people in front of and around her. Out of her silent world and into a Tower of Babel and into Mother's words spattering at her again, "And then, for God's sake, a convent!"

Alma pulled the directions from her pocket. The dean's letter fell out and fell in the snow. She leaned down and picked it up. She dried it off and opened it. A bit wet, but it could still be read. "We have your resume . . ."

Pretty sketchy, except for all those degrees that Mother thought were useless. "First a bilingual secretary that might have at least gotten you a job, and then that BA in some dead language, and forget that, an MA or whatever in what was that? Creative what?"

"We'd like to interview you. Please come to the office of Dean Straven . . . something on January 2 at 2:30 p.m. We have a sudden opening. The position is for tenure, in spite of your terminal degree being what it is. However, the terminology will be Certification of Continuing Employment, and your file must be as complete as the file would be if for tenure, and you will have to enroll in a PhD program as soon as feasible, even though you do have a terminal degree."

She stuffed the letter in her pocket and opened the directions she had evidently wadded in the palm of her hand. She looked at them, stared at them as though she were not staring at them, but knew what they said and why she had them in the first place.

She stared at the Boulevard—six lanes of a wide Sargasso Sea. She should cross it and go in that building that has that sign: "Cardenias Community College." *C'mon, cross it, Alma. If I could live in a tiny dwelling in the sea . . . But you can't, Alma.*

Chapter 16

Sure, the man had been nice. Friendly. Like a *tio*. Telling him, like all the others, no English no job. How many now? Eight? The eighth body shop that had a "mechanic wanted" sign on it.

He walked, letting his fingers slide along the cement side of the building. Now heavy footsteps were behind him. He walked faster.

"Hey, kid."

He kept walking.

"I said, 'hey, kid!' Come here."

He kept walking. He understood c'mere.' Maria said it when she wanted him to wash the dishes. And she was always wanting him to wash the dishes and take out the trash, clean up. That wasn't why he came to the city of the money. And besides, wasn't all that her job? And why is there a white hand on his shoulder. He'd better stop walking.

"I know you don't know English, but you know I'm yelling at *you!*"

He had better stay still with a white hand on his shoulder and an American talking to him.

"You playin' hooky?"

"*¿Qué es* hooky?"

"That be exactly what I mean. Know why I don't give you a job, kid? English! Learn it!"

Now some ass that wouldn't give him a job was telling him what to do!

"Where do you live? Get yourself in school."

That was more English than he could deal with.

He began walking again.

"You go to school and learn English and then come back to this here garage, and you gotta job, okay? I'll give you engine work after school, okay? You look like a good kid, smart, you know? You look smart, but you gotta know how to talk, right? Do you know what I say?"

That was way too much English, but, yes, he sort of knew what the man said. He said what Maria said, "Learn English. Then work."

He looked at the man in the face. He nodded. That should get rid of him.

The man took his hand off his shoulder.

¡Bueno! Now he could get away.

But the man got in front of him. He had to stop, or else bump him.

"Go to the school on the Boulevard. *Go to school, eskayla!*"

Yelling in his face like that he should punch him. No, he's stopping yelling and looking down and looking sad. No, he shouldn't punch him.

They both stood silent.

Should he say a prayer?

The man took a pencil from his pocket and leaned down and picked up a piece of paper from the sidewalk. He wrote.

He watched.

Now the man's handing him the paper and saying, "Go to this school, eskayla. Lake Boulevard and Pike Street. Its new, a new school. One for you guys. Part of a new citywide system. Never mind all that, just go. This here is the name of the dean. Ask for him. Comprendo? I mean, *comprendez?*"

44

No, but he took the paper. This guy couldn't even speak Spanish right, but he should be polite. "*¡Gracias!*" He looked at the paper. It had two words on it.

"That's the name, the name of the dean."

"*¡A Sí!* Llamas!"

"Yeah, yamma."

"*Gracias.*" The man had given him a name. He had a name in his hand.

He knew Pike Street. The hospital was on it. And maybe there was a diesel garage there. One he missed.

He looked at the paper again, and at the man who was standing in front of him still, staring at him, making his eyes go into his head, making him have to say magic words so he would stop. Maybe if he thanked him again! "*¡Gracias!*"

The man nodded and stepped away from in front of him and disappeared.

"*¡Bien dia!*" he yelled back to the man, who maybe would be his new—his real—guardian angel! The paper stuck to the palm of his hand, a lining. He opened up his hand and looked at the name indenting itself into his palm: Robert Stravronousky. Didn't he know all the American names? He never saw a long one like this though.

He stepped off the curb and walked across the street between cars, both stopped and moving, and turned the corner without stepping back onto the sidewalk. If he passed a motor place, he'd stop there first. And he'd try harder in English. He'd say, "There is a motor diesel garage?" No, that wasn't a question. How did Mario ask questions? "Hey, bro, ya gotta . . ." "Hey Maria, ya gonna give me a kiss?"

So a question started, "Ya gotta" or "Ya gonna," not "There is." When he asked for work, it should be "Ya gotta job?" So it was "Ya gotta motor diesel . . . job?" No! "Establishmente." Okay. "Ya gotta motor diesel establishmente *aquí* . . . *aquí* . . . here?"

There! He knew what to say. Happy, happy, happy, he was happy. Lake Boulevard swam in front of him, a great, giant, sun-soaked ocean of cars and noise.

He walked fast, the English singing in his head. "Ya gotta motor diesel establishmente aquí. . . here?"

He came to a lot with a high wooden fence around it that was covered with drawings and glistening signatures, lots of English motherfuckers and other fucks, and even sentences. Spanish sentences too. "*Los Dominicanos son unos vividores.*" "*Las Puertoriquenas son unas iguarantes y putas.*" And rusty pieces of cars lying dead.

He kicked the fence and pounded his fist on the sentences. At least Mario's street was clean and had people living on it. Even if they didn't leave their doors open like in PR. Why did he leave that warm place in the sun with nobody closing their doors and Grandmami holding him on her lap and Mami singing to him to go to sleep? Barranquitas, his home, with mountains all round, hills protecting his town, snuggled like a baby between them? Because he's grown up now, that's why. But does he have to be a grownup in a dirty, mean place like this?

"Hey, man, wear a hat here. Then if somebody hit you on the head at least you has a hat on."

He turned around, his fist up.

"Take it easy—*muchocito cojelo suavesito*—I be you friend, man, *amigo, amigo.*"

He put his fist down. What was he saying about a hat? First Mario said about shoes—wear them. Now it's a hat, something about a hat. But where did the *amigo* go? Gone. Just gone.

CHAPTER 17

Alma crossed the street and stepped on the curb and in back of a moving truck that had scrawled on the side "Nunca Solito," whatever that meant, and that seemed to not care that she was in its way.

"*Watch out, lady!* Yeah, you! Can't you see I'm backing up?"

"Yes." Oh, it did care. *Do not be disturbed by the drama. Have no intercourse with the people of this world . . .*

"Don't just stand there then. I not got all day." The truck jerked.

For little by little you will get a taste . . . for their habits.

She stared at the truck and watched as the back end of it came toward her, open with the sun wavering and weaving over chairs. She took small jumping steps to the side, as stacks and stacks of chairs layered like linen shook.

***

How did he end up here? In front of a school. Yeah, it was Pike Street and the Boulevard like the man said. But no motor place? Where was he ever going to find another motor place? He'd leave and go back to Barranquitas. He'd had enough of Maria and her "c'meres" anyway. No, here he was in front of a school, and what? Walking into the backend of a truck. Maybe he should watch where he was going and not get hit by a truck with

"Nunca Solito" written on the side and moving up the curb and over the sidewalk right toward him—and what was in the truck that should never be alone? With its back end open, gaping, a hole as big as a night sky, filled with chairs, fitting together like lovers. And what is that woman doing jumping back and forth, and the driver yelling at him, "Hey, kid," and that lady in the way.

***

Alma bumped into a young man, said "excuse me," and jumped a few more steps. He nodded. The driver stuck his head out of the window and called, "Hey you, kid. Give me a hand, okay?" The young man said something in Spanish to the driver, who stopped the truck and opened its back door and answered him in Spanish.

***

His guardian angel, his saint, must have led him here without letting him pass a "mechanic wanted" sign, because *that* must be what he was supposed to do—go to school—*pero* he can say no to this angel who's not minding his own business, and now this driver wants him for something.

Alma watched the two of them walk around to the back of the truck and stare at that kaleidoscope of stacked chairs.

"I got lots to take in. Here. Youse a big, strong guy. Spanish, my boss he thinks I know Spanish. You understand me? Here, I gotta get these goddamn chairs in the school!"

Chairs landed on his shoulders. "Follow me."

"Eh!" He's beckoning. He must want him to help carry the chairs in the school. If he did that, it *really* meant he was in the school.

"Over here, Bud, so we don't have to go through that scanning line to just get these chairs inside."

"Huh?"

"*Aquí, aquí. La puerta . . . aquí.*"

Is this another guardian angel telling him to go to school?

The chairs hugging his shoulders swayed, but then settled easily on him. He followed this new guardian angel.

***

Alma watched them lift four at a time from the inside of the truck, hoist them, and turn them into antelope horns. Then, with the chairs on their shoulders, they carried them into the building. She went into the building after them, folding the directions as she went, putting them into her handbag, a final satisfactory finish, she thought, to an interesting interlude. She had conquered two first-worldly dramas.

***

"Thanks for helping with the chairs, Bud. Now, better go in the right way! No, over there in that door! This here's the maintenance door. Unless you work here? Nah, you a new student, I can tell. So, go over there in that door. Where that lady's goin' in. Her. Follow her."

This guardian angel is pointing to another door. Telling him to go to school? Okay. Is this the school his garage man was talking about? The guardian angel's fault. He'll go in, 'cause the angel is telling him to.

Chapter 18

"So they hired you for the English Department?"

"Yes, Professor Comen, the dean—"

"Why ever the dean okayed you, I don't know. I know he's desperate for new faculty—seems no one is applying—but, at any rate, here you are. And I guess I'd better get used . . . I did some investigating, and you haven't even published, so—"

"Actually, I have, a poem in a literary—"

"You call that publishing? But you were hired for remedial writing, right? So now why is the department giving you to me? I'm the ESL supervisor, not the freshman comp supervisor. I was not even at the hiring of you. Do you know our students here? I doubt you'll make it, from the looks of you. Do you speak Spanish? Probably not. But come in and we'll talk, since you *are* hired."

Our labor here is brief, but the reward is eternal . . .

"Thank you, Saint Claire."

"My name is not Claire, as you know. It's Professor Comen. Now, tell me where you live and I'll drive you home, and we'll talk on the way. I want to hear about your experience with our type of student, about what you told the hiring committee, to which I was not invited."

"I'm sorry you weren't there, Professor Comen. I believed I was applying to the English Department myself. However, the students I have taught have been diverse and . . . the Tower of Babble was often prominent."

"And what does that mean?"

Every creature of the world will raise our hearts to God if we look upon it with a good eye.

"Sorry, I didn't hear you. You do mumble. That will not do in the classroom, you know."

"Yes, I am aware of that. I will be careful to keep my voice raised."

***

"Here's my car. This is the official parking place, and be sure to lock your car and take the battery out, and of course be sure your valuables are—"

"I don't have a car. I'll be taking the subway."

"Oh. If you have night classes, be careful. Now, my first suggestion is, since you are a neophyte, there are a few—"

The past must be abandoned to God's mercy, the present to our fidelity.

"There you go again! Muttering under your breath. That just will *not* do in the classroom. Seat belt clipped?"

Alma fastened her seat belt.

"Good. Now, let's see . . . my question, yes, is how did you get all those degrees if you were in a nunnery?"

"I got them before."

"Yes, I see. But one I see is an MFA, maybe terminal, yes, but I'd say useless for this type of teaching. So be it. I think a good initiation would be for you to take an eight a.m. class, which would most likely be young—just out of high school, that is— along with the evening class, which I will give you also, where the students are more mature. That will give you a double taste, I mean a double base."

Close your ears to the whisperings of hell and bravely oppose its onslaughts.

"There you go again, mumbling. Did you hear anything I said? Or am I wasting my breath counseling you?"

"I was just thinking of Saint Claire for some reason. But, yes, I was listening to you, and whatever schedule you give me will be fine."

"With your obvious ignorance of this culture, don't be surprised if you do not make it here."

Alma sat in the front seat of Professor Comen's car and heard her out of one ear talking about the necessity to understand the culture, the hopes and dreams of her Latino youth, and that she, Alma Hedman, being pristine white and ignorant, would have difficulty. And out of the other ear and eye she saw herself standing on the hard-packed earth outside of St. Beggia's waiting for her mother, who was taking forever to pick her up, and was seeing how the tip of her umbrella had sunk into the earth in spite of it being hard-packed and unyielding, and when she did come, her unending chant, "Can't you ever finish anything, Alma?"

"Where are you living, by the way? Here I am driving into the city, and you haven't told me where to take you." Professor Comen's hands clutched the steering wheel, making the veins rise and look wriggly.

"The corner of Sixtieth and Columbus will be fine."

Here you are, no clothes, no house, no job, no . . . Now you have to start from the beginning, and don't you dare start quoting saints to me, and put the umbrella in the back.

"That's a cathedral." Professor Comen's hands were hugging the steering wheel like it would get away from her and stop steering.

"Yes, an Episcopal one," Alma said, staring at the hand on the wheel.

"I thought you said you were no longer a nun."

"I'm not. But you can let me off here. It's near enough, Professor Comen, and thanks."

"Why are you living in a cathedral, or, it's a convent too, I assume?"

"They rent rooms."

Saint Margaret turned into a dragon and then Satan swallowed her.

"I didn't hear you."

The car screeched to a stop, and Professor Comen said, "I'll see you bright and early tomorrow. You will do Registration in Building Two."

"Thanks so much for the ride."

"Your schedule will be in your in-box. And I suggest you curtail that mumbling."

"Yes, good night," she said between clenched teeth.

I drive all the way out here to get you, and all you ever say is how saint so and so was martyred or burned up like a marshmallow or. . .

"I'll do better, Mother."

"I'm not your mother, and like I said, don't forget to look for your schedule. And like I said, too, stop the mumbling."

"Yes, yes, of course, Dr. Comen."

The devil does not sleep, but seeks our ruin in a thousand ways.

Chapter 19

"Hey, Buddy, get in line. You gotta be scanned."

Some *hombre* talking to him?

"Yeah, you! You in the yellow jacket and PR hat. Belts off, pockets out. Gotta get scanned, ya know."

"Scanned? *¿Qué es?*"

"*Aquí . . . haz cola conmigo. Puedes meterte delante mi. ¿Ves aquel hombre alla? Es el* scanner. *Sabes, para armas y cosas . . . cuchillos.*"

And he has to get it explained to him by some girl with big bosoms, and he doesn't have any of that what she said on him anyway. Why would he?

"*¡No ese!*" But it was nice to have someone talking to him in *his* language for a change.

"I know you no got guns and knives and stuff, but they not know. They have to check."

What happened to her Spanish? Why'd she stop talking in it? Why'd she drop it in the ocean for a fish to eat and change to English?

"Next!"

"You . . . *tu . . . vente!*"

There was her Spanish again. Nice how she picked it up before the fish got it.

"By the way, *cómo sé llama?*"

"Carmelo."

"I'm Nurys. See ya."

"Up with your arms, Bud." A policeman? No, some sort of guard raising his arms like in a stretch and looking at him like he should do that too.

So he did. And felt hands go up and down his sides. Right. Like in the airport.

"Okay, Bud. You can go on in."

So this was his school? A fortress, *¡El Moro, El Queda!* So, a war inside? And he was going to be in the army in there? And where was she, that beautiful girl who spoke Spanish to him? Nurys. Yes, Nurys, that was her name.

***

Somewhere in his pocket is that name that guy gave him that time, before he ended up in front of this school by mistake. Here. Here it is.

He un-wadded the piece of paper and showed it to a man standing by the door. The man looked at him in the eyes. Was he giving him the eye?

"Do you speak English?"

He looked at the man in *his* eyes and nodded his head. Then he looked away and shook his head.

"Mr. Stravronousky's office is on the second floor. Go up the up staircase over there, and go to the main office, Room Twenty-Three. This name will be on the door. He's the dean. Understand?"

He did not, but he nodded his head and started toward the stairs that he thought the man had pointed to. He smoothed the paper with his thumb and stared at it while he climbed the stairs.

"Hey, watch where you going."

"*¿Cómo?*" He looked up, and there was that most beautiful girl who had just gotten him through the line to El Moro, standing on the step right above the one he was on and staring down at him.

"This here's the down staircase," she said.

"*¿Qué?*" Didn't she speak Spanish? She did outside.

"I said . . ." She put her hand on his shoulder and turned him around. They both went down the two steps to the floor.

That was nice. *Muy simpatico.* But wasn't he supposed to go to the second floor?

"*Es de la baja* stairs. If you wanna go up, go up over there. *Vente de la arriba* ones. Over there. I'll show you. You're new, obviously. Follow me."

He followed this beautiful girl across the hall and up another set of stairs. Dark hair filled her neck. Wait, no. She was not as pretty as his Miguelina. Dark hair fills *her* neck too, and even falls down her back a ways, and her face is beautiful, like a Barranquitas mountain rose.

Chapter 20

"Here is your class schedule, Professor Hedman. Classes start Monday. And good luck. Believe me, you'll need it. We've never had a nun teaching here."

"Professor Comen, as I mentioned the other day, I'm no longer a nun."

"Yes, yes, you did tell me. But tell me, did they excommunicate you? Is that why?"

"No, they did not. I . . . wanted . . . to be in the world."

"So you chose us to be your guinea pigs? Is that it?"

"I did not think—"

"I'm keeping you. You'd better get back to registration here. I imagine someone showed you the registration ropes so you know what you're doing on the computer. It's new to us, and we are still learning, and it's probably even much newer to you, having been cooped up in a convent all these many years."

Alma looked at the line in front of her and silently thanked Sister Lucy for her intensive computer lessons and said, "Next, please."

All the ways of the world are as fickle and unstable as a sudden storm at sea.

Chapter 21

"Good morning, young man. May I see your ID?"

"*¿Qué es?*" Nobody said "Carmelo, you need to have ID."

"ID? Your driver's license? Guess not. Any ID?"

"ID, *¡Sí!*"

Where was that ID card? He hit his jacket up and down. He hit his pants on the side and in the back. He felt inside his jacket. "Ahhh. *Aquí. Es en mi,*" he said and handed the card to this new guard, all the time thinking why didn't Mario tell him he would have to prove who he was!

"Thanks. *Gracias.* Over there. Room Eighteen. That's what you want if you're new. The dean's office."

He walked down a hall between walls covered with cracked paint. "Ahhh, Room Eighteen."

He opened the door. A girl behind a desk looked up at him. Pretty. He handed the paper with that *loco* name on it to her. She nodded, stood up, and opened another door. She put just her head through that door and let her pretty behind stay back in the room. She said something, then "*estudiante nuevo,*" and brought her whole body back into the room.

"Okay, you can go in. The dean *dice entra.*"

She didn't sound Spanish, but maybe the dean was. No, not with a name like Stravronousky.

He walked around the girl's desk, watching her sit back down, and went into the dean's office.

"What can I do for you, young man?"

"*Quiero classe en* fit motors."

"*Habla inglés, por favor.* Please speak English to me, young man. I may speak Spanish, but you are here for English. Now, let's choose your courses. You may take some in Spanish until you have enough English to mainstream."

Mainstream? Like the Hudson River?

"Obviously, first level for English?"

"*Yo* no took English a fit a motor diesel." Hey, he said it in English, but the dean isn't happy. He's holding his chin with both hands.

"If you want to fix diesel motors, then go to a vocational school and you can learn how to repair televisions too. There is no course here in motor repair. If you think you know English well enough to learn math in it, or history, or social studies, then tell me that you do and say it in English."

That was too much English for him, and he slumped in a chair. He watched the dean write a list of something on a piece of paper. The dean handed it to him and said, "Take this down to registration."

He took it, said "*Gracias,*" walked out through the first door, looked at the girl behind the desk, and tried to make her look like Miguelina.

Chapter 22

"Fifty-two!"

"Fifty-two? *Es mio.*"

Carmelo waved his number in front of the guard and went to where the guard pointed. He sat down between students and across from a row of endless computers with endless teachers behind them. He tapped his knees and he tapped the side of the chair. He got up. He kicked the chair. It folded flat.

Somebody yelled "Calm down!"

He picked the chair up and sat down.

He heard again, "Fifty-two."

"*¡Es mio!*" he yelled, and got up and walked up to a computer that must have been the one to say "fifty-two." He shook the printout that the dean had given him at the computer and the teacher behind it. He hit the top of the computer. "*Es incorrecto.*"

"Why?"

"*¿Porque?*"

"Yes, por kay."

"No motor diesel."

"I'm not sure what you mean."

"*¿Qué?*"

"Do you mean you want a course in repairing cars?"

"*¡Sí, sí!* En fit motors."

"Habla English, por favor. Please speak in English to me. I don't speak Spanish. And sit down."

"Oh shit." Carmelo got up.

"Sit down. *¿Sientese?* Is that how you say that? Sit down. The schedule you have been given will teach you English, and besides, there is no program in repairing cars. No *programa*."

He'd figured that out, but the only way they'd ever have a program in that was if people asked for it. And this teacher had nice eyes, so maybe she could do something about it. She smelled nice too. Sweet, sweet perfume . . . no plain, just right. "*¿Cómo sé llama?*"

"My name? Is that what you are asking?"

"*Sí.*"

"I'm Professor Hedman. Yours, I see, is Carmelo Rogriguez."

"*Sí.*"

"And before I register you for the program you've been given, I need to see your ID."

Again? He pulled out his wallet. She can see his name right there on the paper, and he told her, so why does she need to see his ID too?

He opened his wallet. Not in there. He'd had it before. He put his wallet back in his pocket. He hit his jacket, up and down over his other pockets. He hit his pants on the side and in the back. He stood up. He walked along the line looking in people's hands, careful not to touch anyone.

"*¿Ninguna ha mi documentos?*" He looked at some faces looking at him. "*¿Ay alguin qué tienes mis documentos?*" he said to the faces.

"What's this?" One of these faces was right next to his and was pointing to his pocket. "What's this?" this person said again, and pulled a card out of his pocket. This person was handing his card to him and saying "Is this what you be looking for?"

"*¡Ahhhhhhhh, Dios mio! Gracias, gracias.* Thanks!" Carmelo walked back to where he had been, but someone else was in that seat now. In his place.

"Fuck!"

Alma looked away from the student she was registering and at the student who was using such foul language. Yes, he had been next, and he had gotten up. "You will have to wait, young man," she said to him and turned back, saying to the student in front of her, "Let's see. Where were we?" which blended into Carmelo's second "fuck," noticing at the same time that the only spot in an ESL class was in her class, and that was clearly where the swearing student belonged.

***

"Ah, just the person I want to see. Looked for you in your office, and your office mate, Professor Delores Smith—I believe that's her name?—said you were doing registration. May I interrupt for just a moment?"

The dean? Is he talking to her? *And keep your napkin ring as a reminder of your celestial sojourn* . . . Alma twirled the napkin ring hanging around her neck, her talisman of silence, looked at the student she was about to register twitching like a flickering candle, and said, "Patience is a virtue. I'll have to ask you to wait another moment." She looked up at the dean.

"Yes, you, Professor Hedman. Your chairperson has recommended you . . . has extolled your . . . your talent with words, so to speak."

Chairperson? Or supervisor! Certainly not supervisor. Who has . . . ?

"Your supervisor, Professor Comen, is doing you a favor. She said you needed to start on your personal file immediately and that this would be a good place for you to begin. Please come to my office as soon as you are . . . When are you released from your registration tour of duty?"

"Four o'clock."

"I'll see you then. It has to do with the upcoming self-study, the periodic review report. You are familiar with that, aren't you? Well, no, you might not be, since I don't think you were on the staff yet when I referred to it at the stated faculty meeting last spring. We need . . ." He turned around, causing the last words to trail off into a line of students.

Alma looked at the waiting twitching student who flipped his ID card in the air, caught it between two fingers, and pointed it at her. She said, "Just a minute while I print out your class schedule." She took his card, compared it with the printout, and then handed it to Carmelo, saying, "You are all registered now, Carmelo. Here are your courses."

He took it and mumbled "Shit." Alma watched him fold it into an airplane, raise his arm, and send it soaring into the air ahead of him.

A man who governs his passions is master of the world.

Chapter 23

"Welcome, students. I am Professor Hedman, and I am pleased to be the instrument of learning for you as you embark on your journey of learning what is a new language for you." Alma looked at rows of staring faces and had the feeling she had just spoken to herself.

Build yourself a cell in your heart and retire there to pray.

"That is, let me say this. Your class will be conducted entirely in English, since Spanish is a language I do not know." The staring faces made faces, but then turned their attention to the door. She looked to see what they were looking at, and saw a young man peering through the small window in the top of the door.

The door opened a crack, and then shut. The students giggled.

The door opened again into a much larger crack, and shut. A student shouted toward the door, "*Es uno brujo que no peude make up el mindo.*"

The students laughed, and the door opened wide, and Carmelo stepped inside.

Alma stepped from behind her desk and walked toward Carmelo. "And did you knock first, young man?"

"*¿Qué es* knock?" he said, and handed her his paper airplane.

She took the airplane. Carmelo made a fist and hit the door. Behind her, Alma heard, "*Loco ... violenta ... enfadado.*"

"Come here, Carmelo, and sit," she said.

Carmelo watched her flap her hand toward a desk and chair. C'mere? Like Maria? Flapping her hand at the dishes and saying "c'mere"?

"Come, Carmelo, and sit . . . in the first row here by the door. Next to this young lady." She pointed to the chair and wondered why his grin.

He walked over and sat down. The same? Yes, the same. Nurys. And staring at him. Making her eyes love notes. Yes. "*Muy bonita*," he whispered. But . . . but not half as pretty as Miguelina. What was she doing in this no-speaking-English class? She spoke English earlier.

"Carmelo, you are here just in time. I'm starting the lesson, which, ladies and gentlemen, is the present tense. I am, you are, he/she is, we are, you are, they are. This is a conjugation. Repeat after me. I am . . ."

"Um . . . Nurys," he whispered again. "*¿Por qué estas en la clase de Inglis?*"

"No talking, please. Carmelo, I can give you another seat."

That he understood. "No, no, Professora. No *otra. Es bueno.*" He must have said it loudly, because the whole class looked at him and laughed. But a friendly laugh. Maybe this was not El Moro. And it is good. Here he is next to this friendly, pretty Nurys.

¡Es bueno! ¿En clase mismo?

"*Sí.* You just here? To New York? *¿Aquí?* Just *ayer?* Hey, what's that sticking out of your pocket?"

Why is she speaking English?

"No, *semana . . . dos, tres semana . . . pasada,*" he whispered back.

Alma looked at her new student and his seat mate and put her finger on her closed, pursed mouth. "Silence, postulants, silence," she whispered to her finger.

Carmelo noticed his teacher holding her finger against her mouth and heard her say something, but Nurys was so pretty that he had to pay attention to her. She was talking to him, but again in English.

"So you not here long. So you don't know things, do you? Like that candy bar in your pocket. Better not eat it. You could get a hundred dollars for that . . . for that Blossom Bar! Where'd you get it?"

What is she talking about? "*¿Qué?*" Oh. The candy bar. Maybe she wants it.

He took it from his pocket and put it down on her desk. "*¿Este?*"

"No, no. Quick. Don't let anyone see it. And whisper."

"*Qué es* whisper?"

"It means shhhhhhh."

"*¿Habla Inglés?* Porque you en mismo English like me?"

Alma pointed toward Nurys and Carmelo and said the two words that her new officemate had taught her. "*¡Silencio por favor!*"

"Shhhhhh! You make trouble. We talk after class."

Alma picked up a piece of chalk. "The present tense, boys and girls, that is where we shall start."

Nurys cupped her hand over her mouth and said, "'Cause I need English. We gotta learn that grammar."

Alma turned around. "Nurys, Carmelo, please. *¡Silencio por favor!*"

Nurys picked up the candy bar and stuffed it back into Carmelo's pocket. "Carmelo, it's a drug," she whispered. "Get rid of it." She patted his pocket where she had stuffed it.

"Carmelo, *do not* respond to Nurys. The present tense, children, is *now*."

Oh, maybe she does want it. Carmelo pulled the candy out of his pocket and laid it on her desk.

"No, no!" She threw it onto his desk. "Hide it, dummy. Here comes la professora."

"*Qué* 'hide'? *¿Dice en Español*, okay?"

Nurys pushed it back into his pocket, and again shoved it way down.

Alma walked toward their desks. "Carmelo and Nurys! What is going on?"

"See? Now you got us in trouble. Nothing, Professora. We friends."

"Time for silence. Time for silence while we talk about *now*."

Alma walked back to the front of the room, picked up a piece of chalk, and wrote: "THE PRESENT TENS—" On the *E*, the chalk broke.

Chapter 24

INTRODUCTION

In synchrony with the establishment of the Great University's Ad Hoc Committee of Multilingual Educational Considerations of the Advisory Sub Committee on Special Pedagogical Issues, *such as Carmelo's interest in repairing motors,* and the resulting policy of the need for bilingual classes, Cardenias Community College became *Carmelo's initiation into a new culture's idiosyncrasies and strange habits and* an oasis of learning in an area of the city devoid of such a life-giving need and opened its doors after five years of negotiations, trials and errors, a time in which accreditation occurred, albeit provisionally until the making of this current report *and Carmelo helped carry in the chairs.* A warehouse is this current educational haven for *Carmelo and other* residents of East Park and other similar communities, providing opportunities leading toward socio-economic mobility.

Alma slammed her finger on the mouse and concentrated on directing the curser in the right direction, with her eye on her notes. She stared at the scribblings tucked between the laptop and the lamp.

The notes blurred and Carmelo swam again to the surface. She probably should not have sat him that first day next to that student with the name Nurys, a name she had no idea how to pronounce, but guessed anyway, and it was right evidently, because Nurys did not correct her the way Mercedes had corrected her when she pronounced her name "Mercado." Yes, she should have sat him next to a boy.

Chapter 25

"Hi, Carmelo. That candy bar's still stickin' outta your pocket? Are you nuts? *¡Loco, loco, loco!*" Nurys kicked a beer can into the curb, then stepped onto the blacktop of Capa Park.

Nurys! How nice. How did she know where he was? Did she follow him after class? Did she watch him, and he didn't know it?

"Where do you live, Carmelo?"

"Barranquitas." He watched her shadow wiggling next to her like a snake, dropped there probably by the afternoon sun and sitting on his thigh like it owned it.

"No, *no*, dummy! Now *ahora, aquí?*"

"Oh. *En Nueva Yorka?* One . . . five . . . nine . . . um . . . Street. *Una* . . . one . . . subway . . . station . . . a *aquí.*"

"Great. Near my uncle! I talk to him about you. That maybe you want a job con he, like, you interested in any extracurricular activities?"

"*¿Qué?*"

"You know. Like that Blossom Bar that, like I say, is still stickin' outta you pocket. If you gonna keep it, at least better hide it, but keep it low in you pocket." She pushed it further down into Carmelo's pocket, which sent her hand down his leg, and he jumped. She pulled her hand back out and sat down next to him.

"And like I already say, not for you to eat, but maybe sell it and then get people to buy. Hey, you can even get some stuff for me to sell if you want. Just don't *you* eat it or you get addicted. And I be here for you. *Mi tio*, like I say, he's discreet. That you gotta learn, to be discreet. And you need to try to talk in English, or you'll not never . . . I mean, *ever* learn it. *Jamas* . . . know what I said? Just now?"

"*Sí.*" She said what he guessed everybody said.

"So, from now on—English!" she said, poking at his pocket. "*Mi tio*, he have stuff like that that'll make you feel good. And you can sell too."

"Feel good?"

"Yeah, feel. Feel . . . like this."

Now she's rubbing her hand on his cheek, and his leg is still jumping a little. He put his hand on his thigh to make it stop. He looked at the sun that was now on his hand, and thought of Miguelina.

"Feel? Feel good? *Bueno?*" She smoothed his cheek.

"Ahhhhhhh." *Pero Mguelina es mi amor.* "No." He took her hand off his cheek and put his own hand in his pocket.

"I'm talking about pot, dude. Not just love, but that too, of course. And why you move my hand? My uncle, near you, he has it all going real good. I know. I'll tell Tio you'll meet him here, and away from the school, but tell him you from me 'cause he gives me a exclusive commission."

Was she offering him a job too, like Rudolfo? Here he was just looking for a place to be still and quiet and figure out if he should stay in this college or try another job place, and as soon as he sits here in the quiet, she is picking at his life. Rudolfo is not the kind of job place he wants.

"No, Nurys, *no quero trabajo con ese.* I no interesting—"

"Good! You used English. At least one word. But say 'interested,' not 'interesting,' in that sentence. Tambien, maybe you not interested now, but you will be. I know so. By the way, this good place to meet. How did you find this place? All by itself. Sort of hidden-like. And not *too* garbagy. Want to meet here every day after class? We can talk, or we can … we can even make out. Do you know a word I just said? No, course not. That's why I could say it to you, dummy. You better learn English fast, or you miss a lot. Or you get taken, or … I know. I'll teach you English this way: *besame, besame mucho cómo…*"

He pushed her mouth away, stood up, and started walking out of the park. She stood up and walked next to him. They walked along the wide sidewalk, stepping between and over soda cans, pieces of paper, dog stuff—none of this in his home city—and Nurys isn't even noticing it at all.

She stopped walking and stepped in front of him, stopping him, rubbed her hands through his hair, and said, "You have nice hair. The kind what a girl wants to—"

"Ahhh." *Pero Miguelina es mi amor.* "No. *Mi amor es en—*"

"If we gonna be any kinds friend, you gotta talk in English, you know, 'cause I try to get away from my Spanish. It's what my father yells at me all the time. Anyway, when you do need stuff, or want, or need to sell candy bars to somebody or anything, I'm here for you … and for anything else you want too. *Cómo …besame.*"

Carmelo flung his arms back as Nurys' tongue sank into his mouth. She slowly pulled it out, lathered his lips, and let her tongue slide down his chin, then moved to his ear, kissing it. She stepped away. "Bye."

"*¡O Dio, Nurys! Pero, entendez.*" But she was gone, leaving him with his arms out, with nothing to grab, but … but he needed to tell her that he wasn't so sure about her games. *Malo,* like Rudolfo's.

Except … except at the same time he wanted her to stay forever, that drop of Puerto Rican angel dust. And would there be more? Then no . . . no, Miguelina will be the one to give him ear kisses and lip kisses and more. But Nurys, she'll be good to him in this city.

Maybe Mami was right. He should find his saint.

Carmelo cupped his ear to hold onto the tingling.

Chapter 26

BEGINNINGS

This renovated warehouse at 2989 Lake Boulevard, *where Carmelo nearly ran into the back of a truck, and where, because of that, he was asked to help carry chairs—stacked like layers of linen—into the building and in the process nearly knocked over an ex-nun, and* where the courses, from the beginning, were and have been offered in both Spanish and English, and where gradually, through a period of political and economic strife, administrative readjustment, modification of the college and its curricula took place, *and Carmelo's English teacher was this ex-nun, Professor Alma Hedman, an ex-Episcopalian nun whose perfume, which she did not wear, but which he confused with that worn by the students around him, and, no matter who was wearing it, he was convinced, was leftover incense from the last mass, and this became a loud discussion in Spanish, in which she wished to interject the information that Episcopalians did not spray incense, but the Spanish was such that to introduce English into the discussion would not be appropriate. Some of the Spanish the professor understood, but not enough to make her comments legitimate. She, the professor, was, in conclusion, accused of being obsessed with silence in the classroom.*

Chapter 27

"Wanna ride?"

He ignored the "wanna ride" echoing behind him.

"I said, 'wanna ride'? What you doing, little bro of Mario? Dreamin'? You dreamin'? *Hey! You!* Wake up. I'm askin' you if you want a ride to you school. I'm on my way to you house. We got works to do, you brother and me, but I can take a time and deliver you to you school, what on the way. So . . . so . . . *get in!*"

This voice was coming through a fog. A haze. His ear was still tingling. He did not want it to stop, but some words were spitting through the fog: dreamin', ride, going, get in!

A truck was moving slowly on the street alongside him. He looked at it. In it. Rudolfo? Yes, Rudolfo. Those spat words came from him.

"Get in!" The truck was jerking toward a stop. "Dream boy!"

The truck stopped. The door opened.

Stuck. Felt like he better get in or something bad was going to happen.

"Atta boy. Settle in and we off to your school."

The truck moved. He couldn't get out.

"As I say, Dream Boy."

Qué és 'dream boy'?

"Know what I mean, man? Gotta stop the dream, man. Ya gotta be on my team, man! Ya gotta wean from dream, man, and pay goddamn attention. You know what I mean, or don't ya?"

"*¿Qué?*"

"Oh shit. You don't. I guess I gotta be more *ex*plicit with you. Ya been in school now, enuf what you got friends, 'cause you is a friend-makin' kinda guy, not a dude what's shy. So I gotta idea you be populaaaar in no time, and so in no time we talk about you being my supplyaaaar.

The truck stopped.

"Okay, here you school. I let you out. *Pero*, I see you later."

Carmelo got out of the truck and watched it roll down the street like a lizard on wheels. Whatever Rudolfo was talking about mushed in his head and lodged in a no-English part of his brain.

Chapter 28

INITIAL FACILITIES

This renovated warehouse, *a place where Carmelo has a propensity to be late and to disrupt the class,* at this point, is completely renovated and has been transformed into classrooms, administration areas, and student services areas, and was actually in the process of undergoing a second renovation, starting with new chairs for the repainted classrooms, when funding was suddenly cut, *and if Carmelo's flirtatious nature does not also get nipped in the bud, it might also become a problem.*

Chapter 29

That red truck is pulling to a stop.

"Get in, Mario's little bro."

No, not again.

"Caught ya 'fore ya got to the subway. Ya got a ride to school like before, so get in."

Carmelo shook his head and kept walking.

"Get *in*, 'fore I drag ya in like before."

Carmelo got in.

Rudolfo stepped on the gas. "You got any contacts in that school yet? Do you keep your ears open? You eyes? So you knows what be going on and see who you can trust and who's a po*ten*tial good friend? *Bueno*? Huh? Huh?"

"No. *Sí.* No."

"Make it *sí*. The subject of my idea here is crack. I give you money. You get me stuff. And then I give *you* money, a percent of what I make sellin' what you get me. A percent for *you*! This here a sample. It'll look like this if someone asks for it right. And it won't upset your teachers if they happen to see it, but don't let them, It'll look like a Milky Way to them. You do this, I can expand business, 'cause you'll know all these kiddos in school who'll want it, and they'll know who to go to for it—*you*."

What's he stuffin' in his pocket? "*¿Qué?*"

"Called a Blossom Bar. Look like a candy bar, right? Unless you knows better."

Rudolfo's words cut into him. He should tell him he already had one of those in his other pocket. But maybe Rudolfo would take the one he already had! Nurys said . . . what did she say? Sell or something. She meant he shouldn't keep it.

"Don't forget you get a percent. If you is dee-cent. Hey, I rhyme! You like my rhyming, huh?"

"¿Qué?"

Rudolfo rubbed his fingers together. "Yeah, percent. Money. *Money!* I ain't bein' funny! Ha, Í do it again! Anyway, here you school."

The truck stopped.

"Open the door. Í gotta move. This here a stand-only, and sell what Í give you, hear?"

Carmelo got out. With *malo malo* in both pockets now. Rudolfo must be talking about pesos maybe. He could pay maybe rent then maybe make Mario stop picking on him. But Rudolfo's talking about drug money. Did that mean he was a *traffacaner*? And would that mean that he, Carmelo, was too? No, he was just getting it. That was all. Not using it himself, and just selling this one bar and that would be all. And he would get a percent, which meant money probably, and he could pay rent, send it to Mami, get a plane ticket for Miguelina. No, she wouldn't come here. She was probably right now painting that clay cup with her red crayon, and filling it with honey and oil and azogue, and writing his name on brown paper and putting seven needles on that and putting a glass of water on that and . . . He should have stayed home and become asiento. But how could he do that and be honest? He was no saint.

"Here we is. So, who do ya know?" Rudolfo pulled the truck to the curb and turned off the ignition too fast, before he even put it in park, just like Mario.

"Like I say, who do ya know, little Mario's bro? Don't gotta be a pro, just a guy or gal with a glow. So, out with the name a this pal. I got my hands on you neck, see? So, out with it."

"Okay, okay. Nurys. Yeah, Nurys."

"And do what I say, or you get this." Rudolfo's hand squeezed his neck, but then went back onto the steering wheel. With the other hand, he rubbed his fingers together again, making money out of those fingertips.

Rudolfo es loco.

Chapter 30

Funding

Although funding had been cut due to a state and city financial crisis, readjustment, modification of the college and its curricula continued to take place, *and Carmelo and Nurys left class together just about every day, at least on the days that Carmelo attended class, which were becoming fewer every week, while Professor Hedman juggled two other classes squeezed in twice a week, her schedule having been setup by Professor Comen, one being eight o'clock in the morning and the other being eight o'clock at night, which meant that two days a week she was not at her best and not able to closely monitor whisperings and innuendos between Carmelo and Nurys, which seemed to be sprinkled with words of affection—on Nurys's part—and a particularly oft-repeated name of Rudolfo—mostly on Carmelo's part.*

Chapter 31

Mario grabbed Carmelo's jacket. "*What that fucking thing in you pants pocket?*"

"*¿Qué?*" Now this candy bar is upsetting Mario. Anyway, how did it get to be sticking out like that again. She'd pushed it down. She'd pushed it way, way down, and then tickled him—like before—at the same time, and giggled.

"*Este . . .* this." Mario pulled it out and waved it in front of his face. "*Dónde? Quién?* Where you got it?"

"Rudolfo. *Dice* is candy bar."

"It ain't no Mars Bar or Hershey Bar or Butterfinger. It ain't at the news counter with the *news*papers. It ain't sitting side by side with the *Daily News* and *El Dario*, and you no get it from Rudolfo. Rudolfo no have time or money for this stuff. If you startin' to deal, if you is gonna be a traffacaner, you is goin home to Mami, not in *my* house. So you go get it back to whoever asshole gave it to you, *oiteh?* Hear me? *And* I expecting that rent, or you goin' home for not paying me that!"

"*Pero no trabajo.*"

Mario threw the candy bar in the trash, turned his back, and left the room.

Carmelo picked it up out of the trash and put it back in his pocket. Rudolfo would want to know where it was and if he had sold it yet, so how could he say Mario threw it away?

Chapter 32

Budget Cuts

Budget cuts, due to the sudden cut in funding from the state, impacted heavily on Cardenias, thus forcing the college to increase class size, with some classes being held in the hall, which made the use of the blackboard possible only if it were wheeled in from a nearby classroom *and gave Carmelo an uncontrolled urge to take advantage of the proximity of the elevator to make repeated attempts to escape while yelling something to Nurys about her tio meeting him on some corner.*

This necessity forced Professor Hedman to request of her male students help in recruiting blackboards from adjacent classrooms *and Carmelo was frequently dispatched on this errand in order to keep him from bolting from class after a row with Nurys,* and this interruption from productive educational practice resulted in disjointed teaching procedures.

Chapter 33

Alma put her hand on the rubber edge of the subway door, stopped it from closing, and stepped into the car. Might as well be a subway car to hold a class in. *Carmelo, don't you go near that elevator. Awilda, you don't have to say hi to everyone who passes by. Juan, sit up and stop moving your chair closer to the stairs.* At least in a subway car, they'd have to stay in one place.

Alma swayed and grabbed a strap.

I said you'd never understand these students. And moreover, Professor Hedman, in order to come close to getting tenure, you'll need to be enrolled in a PhD program, if you aren't already, and I'm sure you're not, and why they hired you without at least working for a doctorate I don't know.

Is that a hand on her breast? She should cut the breast off and carry it around in a basin like Saint somebody or other. *Act like this isn't happening, Alma. Don't call attention to this. Look down the car in the other direction.* She could yell. *No, don't call attention. When the car stops, move.* Where's her saint when she needs one?

The train stopped. Alma let go of the strap and swatted the air. The hand disappeared into the crowd. *He who desires nothing . . .*

She sat down on an emptied seat. She closed her eyes. Her hall class came before her eyes. Tomorrow the same. The syllabus. What's next on the syllabus? The past tense. A childhood memory.

Here's an example, boys and girls, from my own childhood. I had a friend. She wanted her name changed. It was Carolyn. She wanted it to be Carl, because she wanted to be a boy.

She said, "Baptize me."

I said, "How?"

She said, "Use that old toilet in my basement, but first we'll have a gathering of all Presbyterians and Methodists and Episcopalians and Baptists and Catholics and Congregationalists and Mormons. And then she said yes to the geranium flats. To turning them upside down on big flower pots so the congregation can sit, and yes to the wire frame to make the cross, and plugging the bottom of the toilet with fresh moss.

And that's the font.

Then . . . her hand? So tiny on her breast? So tiny, but there, and it . . . didn't want that hand on it.

The train slowed. Her station was coming up. She stood up, grabbed a strap, and threw her briefcase onto her chest.

He who desires nothing but God is rich and happy.

That should get her through the day.

Chapter 34

"Get in, Dream Boy."

Not again! Here he was, wanting him in the truck again. "No, Rudolfo."

"I got ideas for you and me! And how come this Blossom Bar still be in you pocket stickin' out like a flag, sayin' 'look at me'? I tell you sell it—for practice—remember?"

"No, no. Mario *dice returno*—"

"You leave your bro outta this! What's this returno? This between you and me, see? So I not takin' it back. Like I say, you gotta practice. Here's what you do. I tell you again. You gotta *sell* it, and then when you get good, you find who you can *get* it from. *Comprendez*, little bro? You 'member? You say a Nurys, so be keen and mean and—"

"*¿Cómo? ¿Qué?*"

"Geez, don't be *estúpido*. It be simple. First you sell. You get contacts. *¿Quién sabe?* Nurys? You say Nurys."

"*Sí*. Nurys. *Nurys el dice el tio.*"

"Fantastico. Sell it to Nurys, and then she get her uncle to buy and we go from there, okay? After that it'll be easy. Everybody'll know what they're gettin' and you get the hang a sellin', and I can expand business, 'cause you'll know all those kiddos, not just Nurys, in school who'll want it. But keep it on the street away, not in youse classes, you hear? So, you know the dope and what you doing, and being cool and all that, and don't forget you gets youse percent. And if you teacher see it, it all look like Milky Ways and Happy Days and Pretty Lays. You get it?"

Still bad candy in his pocket? He can't keep both stuffed way down all the time. But . . . money. He needed that all right in this city of the money that isn't the city of the money. There's no gold on these streets like they say at home, so, *Sí*, he could probably do that, even if it did mean he was a traffacaner.

"You dreamin' again? Back to the candy bar . . . you don't eat it, see?"

"No. I no eat. Nurys say—"

"Yeah! Nurys! And her *tio*. So *bueno*, I get back to you in a like *mañana* . . . no, *Lunes*. Give you time, Dream Boy."

"*¿Por que?*"

"To get your contacts, to know Nurys . . . better . . . and her *tio*."

Why? He already knows her. Too well! God, that kiss on his ear. Oh God. Oh God!

"Hear me, little bro?"

Rudolfo's voice in his head shattered that kiss on his ear. "Hear me? By tomorrow."

He should tell Mario what Rudolfo was doing to him, making him go *malo, malo, malo*. Why did he leave that warm place in the sun with Mami singing "*Duermete Mi Niño*" so he could go to sleep?

Chapter 35

"This Nurys, didja juice her up? Didja sell to her? Did you? Like you said you could? Didja? Don't make me have to slug you, you pug you!"

Rudolfo's hand gripped Carmelo's neck. Carmelo moved and felt Rudolfo's fingers go between his muscles. He gagged.

"Answer me! Did you do any a that? Like I told ya to?"

"*Sí.*" Carmelo's yes was weak, but it was a yes, and Rudolfo loosened his hold.

"So's you done went to this chick and you done sell the candy dandy, and where the hell's the money? *Comprendee?*"

"*¿Cómo?*"

"You don't comprendee, do ya, you *loco niño?* You no do that, didja?"

"*¿Qué?* Sell?"

"Yeah, sell."

"She no *quiere.* She—"

"Okay, we do anoder way. This time I give you money so youse can play. You take you money here that I give you, and you give you money to her—or him—and she give it to her source, her tio, and that source, her tio, give her the crack. We do big time. We forget candy dandy, and she give the crack to you, and what percent she get, that her business. And you gets the crack to me, and I gives you a percent so youse pays rent, and you tell Mario next month you give it to him that you has a job. You tell that bro a yours that next month he get rent. Comprendee?"

"*Yo no sé* —" The fingers grabbed and gripped again. "*¡Sí, sí!* I do that. I do that!" He choked out more English words before the grip loosened again, and finally Rudolfo's hand slid off his neck and down his side and into his pocket.

"By tomorrow, you motherfucker. I'm leavin' you now 'til we have our next pow wow!"

Carmelo nodded. Source? That must be her uncle. He'd have to get this crack he talked about from Nurys, but she's making *him* sell this candy bar. Why was she so beautiful? Maybe she wasn't really. Her uncle was careful, she said. How was he supposed to do this? Maybe Nurys wasn't so pretty after all, but she had helped him that very first day when the world was crazy for him, and a friend is a friend.

"No, Nurys, I no interesting," he had said to her in English, and she had said, "*Bueno*, Carmelo, you use English." And then she had rubbed her bosom on his chest and said, "Okay, not now, but if you do . . . I mean, need it or want it."

Chapter 36

What's next? The departments. Need the reports from them for this. This Carmelo is a problem. So is this computer. The keys are sticking. Data Processing didn't clean the keys before bringing it to her. Lucky she had an officemate who had some experience with the new modern world, but where was Delores when she needed her, like, to unstick the keys?

The aforementioned financial crisis reached a crescendo . . .

Already asked the departments once. And what is she supposed to do when Juan or somebody pushes the chalkboard in front of the elevator, obviously with good intentions, but then when somebody gets off it they yell where are they and what floor is this, and she has to run and push it away, and then everybody laughs at her?

"Look the nun. Look, nun run, run, run."

Should she have pointed out that they left out the preposition?

"She no like it joke. She talk preposition."

And the closing of the campus seemed imminent . . .

Chapter 37

"Now you think you is some big hot shit 'cause you in school?" Mario stood on a chair waving a knife. "Well, you ain't."

"You say *el trabajo no*, so I *no trabajo. Yo vengo a la escuela*—like you say."

"I never say you ain't gotta pay me *sompin*—rent or sompin."

Mario sculpted at the air with the knife and Maria screamed. Mario let the knife drop. It went straight down and plunged its tip into the floor. The handle and most of the blade swayed, like a palm branch to a breeze on his Arecibo Beach.

Mario and Maria watched it. When it stopped swaying and only tilted, Mario got down from the chair and hugged Carmelo. Then he said, "Where'd you get those fuckin' bruises on your neck? More fighting in the subway, you goddamn bro?"

"No, no. I—"

"I knows when you lie. Well, here's a punch to go with the bruises."

The punch landed Carmelo on the floor and landed Maria on top of him, with her yelling at Mario.

"Okay, Maria. I's sorry, bro. You can get in fights if you want. And you is right about school. *Vete a la escuela*, I say. Live with us, I say. Okay, yeah, I say that. I say all that. I remember. But business is no good, and I need some rent from you."

He stepped back, letting his arms drop to his side, and said softly, "*Mi hermano, mi hermano, mi hermano de sangre, pero* you gotta get a job!"

Carmelo stood up and leaned against the wall. There were lots of mistakes in his life right now, and coming to live with Mario was one big one. How was he ever going to get money to pay him rent?

Wait! Yes! The percent from Rudolfo. Of course!

In the airport, he'd given Mami a big hug. "You my sweet boy, Carmelo," she'd said. "You my kind, sweet boy. New York City is not a kind, sweet city. Be careful. Don't do wrong. Keep your kind, sweet self, my kind, sweet boy."

Chapter 38

Sell it, yes. He didn't want it in his pocket anymore anyway. And it would shut Mario up.

¿Pero Quién? Ah, the guy at the mechanic place who likes him. He'll do him a favor like this. He can see he knows English now, and so he can give him a job so he doesn't have to be a Rudolfo.

He got on the train, pushing and shoving because now he knew that that was the only way to get on before the doors closed. He grabbed the dangling handle and jerked and swayed with the train's moving and swaying, and watched for the name of the station stop as the train slowed, stopped and started, and slowed and stopped. *Aquí . . . uno cincuenta y* Pike.

He pushed and pushed and got himself onto the platform. He went up the subway stairs two at a time and turned toward Pike Street. Is this the way? Yes, this is the way. Down Pike then over and around that corner. Another block. Here it is.

The good garage man could get him out of this mess. Miguelina could if she were here. Or her uncle could, being asiento, a shining saint in all his white that time when they all decided to do some black magic and her uncle said, "Go to a mayombero if you want evil." So they imitated him doing only white magic, by making a path of stones and egg shells and other stuff all through the woods, but nothing happened, because they weren't asiento. None of them, her uncle said, but Oshun was forgiving. "So, don't worry," he said.

But the garage man is not in that world and . . . um . . . um . . .
he looks busy. *Aquí. Aquí el garage. Entro . . . saludo al jefe. Hablo
Inglés . . . aprendo . . . digo 'Vengo despues de escuela. . . y trabajo.'
Pero en Inglés.* Yes, now I got to say that in English. I come after
school . . . and . . . work.

"*¿Uh, cómo esta?*"

"Hey! My protégé. You in school? Like I sent you? Find Mr.
Stravronousky? Got good classes? Learning English, 'ceptin' you
ask me how I am. Come on, say that in English!"

"Um . . . How—"

"Good, good. But don't come looking for a job 'til you can do
more than 'how.' Then we'll see."

Is he telling him to leave? "Um . . . um . . . no *pregunta*. . .no
job *ahora, pero* I . . . I . . ." What's the word? "Need. *Sí*, need. *Yo*
need—"

"Go on, need what? Besides a job. What?"

Show him, stupid. Just show him what's in your pocket.

He reached into his pants pocket and brought out a Blossom
Bar. "*Este* . . . this."

"Ha! How'd you get that? You with the wrong people? Not
good. You telling me you need to sell it, huh?"

"*Sí, Sí.*"

"Just this once. Then you get other friends, you hear?
'Cause you don't know what you are doin', do you? You ain't
got no idea the trouble you gonna be in, do you? Tell you what.
I'll buy it from you quiet-like here, now, this time, and you
give the guy that gave it to you the money I'm giving you,
and I'll get rid of it for you—and for me—and you don't have
nothing to do with the guy that give it to you to sell. You tell
him you did it and give him this money, like I say, and then
stay *away*, stay *way away* from him, hear me? *¿Comprendo?* I
mean *comprendez?*"

He's doing it. He's buying it from him. He's taking it from him and he's getting money from his pocket and handing it to him. "Do what I say," he's saying to him. "Give this to the guy that told you to sell, hear me?"

Dio mìo. "*Gracias, gracias.*"

"No, don't thank me. Just do what I say."

Uh oh! He didn't tell the man not to eat it. He'd better go back and tell him.

"You back?"

"*Sí. ¡Olvidé decirle no eat ése barra de caramelo!*"

"Thanks, kid. 'Cept I don't know what you just said."

Goddamn, now he'd have to figure out how to say that in English. "You . . . um . . . no . . . um . . . no eat *qué*. No, no eat that . . . that Blossom Bar. It no *es bueno*."

"Wasn't planning to. Told you I'd get rid of it. That don't mean I get rid of it in my stomach. And what the hell's the matter with your neck, all bruised like that? Not gettin' in fights are you? Stay out of fights, you hear? And stay in school."

Okay. He told him, now he could take care of the next step. Whatever it was. Like probably getting rid of Nurys. But how?

***

Carmelo got on the subway. Free—a free man. Nothing in his pockets and some money in his hand. That is being free. That is feeling the world around you like a bubble of joy. He swayed with the train, his arm hanging from the strap like a monkey on a limb. A happy monkey on a limb.

Wait! The money in his hand—the one hanging on—crazy, crazy! How can he be so crazy? Put it in your pocket, dummy, where no one can see it.

Carmelo grabbed a pole, let go of the strap, and put the money in his pocket. Uh oh! Something there already now—besides the money. What?

Carmelo felt. He felt the other something. *Dios mío* —that other candy bar. He should have sold both. And all this money from Rudolfo, like he could ask Nurys for crack?

Carmelo climbed the subway stairs, having tossed his bubble of joy onto the train tracks.

Chapter 39

ADMINISTRATION

The aforementioned financial crisis reached a crescendo, and the closing of the campus appeared imminent, in spite of the steady increase in enrollment and the improvements in the physical structure. But the governor moved in and averted the crisis, and thus put the school on firm financial footing, allowing attention to now be paid to the policies of the administration. The administration is now divided into three areas: (a) Business and Financial, (b) Academic Affairs, including faculty hirings and observations, and (c) Student Services. The various subdivisions of the three administrative areas are shown in the appended charts, *and Mother is still talking in her letters about that hope chest she was filling and how upset the aunts were that their niece did not come home. And Carmelo has stopped coming to school again, and why, her mother would want to know, did that belong in the same paragraph as the fact of her not coming home. Was there some sort of hidden meaning that she was not getting?*

Chapter 40

Carmelo stood outside Room 19 and rubbed his neck. At least class wasn't in the hall anymore and he could stand outside and get himself ready to go in, but how could he hide the bruises on his neck? He was late, but what did that matter after two weeks of not going at all, waiting for the damn bruises to go away and two weeks hiding from Rudolfo. But Nurys . . . he needed to see Nurys.

Was that the roll being called?

"Alejandro Pena?"

And the answers being given?

"*Aquí.*"

And the corrections the teacher was making. "English, please. The word is 'present,' as you know."

"Sorry, Teacher."

And the apologies.

"Awilda Quinones?"

"*Aquí* . . . no, no. Present."

"Good, Awilda. Nurys Reyes?"

"*Presente.*"

"Carmelo Rodriguez?"

"He not here, Teacher."

"Thank you, Nurys."

Yes, he was. Right here. Okay, maybe not in the room, but should he go in?

"Mercedes Sanchez?"

"*Presente.*"

"Yes, present, not *presente.*"

"Sorry, Teacher."

He would have to go in if he was going to get Rudolfo's money to Nurys. So, did he have a choice anyway? No. Either get it or be choked.

"Juan Velez?"

"*Aquí.* Um ... um ... um ..."

Or be dead.

"How many times do I have to tell you to say 'aquí' in English?"

He had better not wait any longer, or he would be interrupting more than just the roll call, and everybody would look at his neck.

He opened the door.

"Hey, Teacher, here he is, that Carmelo kid."

"Thank you, Hector. Come in, Carmelo. Sit down now so that we can begin chronological order, which we will study before I have you write about your first day in New York. This will give you tools like 'then,' 'after that,' 'before,' and 'now.'"

He sat down and nudged Nurys. She nudged him back.

"*Yo tango* ... twenty-five *por* ... *por* ... *you por su tio,*" he whispered.

She smiled and whispered back, "Did you sell—"

"*Sí. Pero no money con ese* ... *tango money para* ... *para su tio. Yo tango para amigo de mi hermano—pero no es mi amigo, pero—*"

"*Nurys? Carmelo?* And you, Carmelo, you cannot afford to ... you have missed two weeks of school."

Alma looked at Carmelo's neck. Something was wrong. Another fight? *Saint Agnes was stabbed in the throat in* ...

"Now, for chronological order, if you are making barbequed pork, *echon asado,* the sequence—the order—of what you do is important, right? Class? Right, Carmelo?"

"*¿Qué?*" He doesn't cook, pork or anything, so why the question?

"I'm only seeing if you are paying attention. You have to follow a recipe, and the order is important. You can't put the cart before the horse. That's an idiom. I'll draw it."

"Teacher Alma *loco*," Carmelo whispered and watched his teacher turn around, walk to the blackboard, and pick up a piece of chalk. Did Nurys hear him?

"Psst, Carmelo, meet me out front after class."

"Do not put the cart before the horse. That's an idiom. I'll draw it."

He watched his teacher write on the blackboard, all the while trying to figure out how to split Rudolfo's money with Nurys—and what did she want him to do with her uncle, wherever he was and whoever he was? What was he going to say to him when he did find him, and why was his teacher drawing a rectangle and circles under the rectangle and saying, "That's a cart. It is going in this direction, to the left"? And drawing a horse with its nose over the back of the cart and . . . Did she see them whispering? No, she was too busy drawing this stupid donkey on the blackboard, swooshing her chalk into a horse and putting its nose over the back of the car and saying, "See? The horse has to go first, not like this. The right order is necessary. "Now, I want you to write. Here is your topic: My first day in New York. And here again are those words of chronological order: first, then, next, and after. Write them down. Use them in writing your memory. Write at least one sentence."

Agnes was stabbed in the throat. Which caused more than a bruise on her neck.

Now he was supposed to write? Wasn't speaking English enough? And wasn't *that* what she was supposed to be teaching? Speaking? And not how to draw a cart in front of a horse?

"We talk after school." Nurys pulled paper and a pencil from her school bag and acted as if she had not said a word.

***

"*Mi tio*. It's my uncle, Carmelo. Wait, let's get away from the building. My uncle sells it, not me. So I tell him, you meet him over there, away from the building, not all the way to Capa Park. That our place. Okay? I tell him, you have fifty for his crack. Then you sell it to you friend."

"I say, he no *mi amigo, y no tango* fifty." He had fifty, yes, but only half was for her, and some for rent.

"Gotta be fifty, Carmelo."

"*En otra time, sí, pero . . . tango mas otra* Blossom Bar."

"What? You have another one? Where did you get . . . never mind. You just gotta get rid a that too. Maybe I help *mi tio*. Gotta go. I see."

"No, no, *entendez*, Nurys." But she was gone. He would throw it away, put it in the trash. Why didn't he think of that before? Because it's money, that's why.

Chapter 41

Alma faced the blackboard. Behind her was a cacophony of Spanish.

She turned and said, "*Silencio, por favor.*" This was her ploy for saying she knew Spanish and would know what they were saying, which of course was not true, but it shattered the cacophony.

She waved the chalk. "One paragraph . . ." this seemed to have more weight than "Silencio por favor," and she continued talking into the now dimming noise, "in which you will tell me about your first day in this country. Last time I wanted one sentence. And, as I recall, I got nothing. So, I will ask again for one sentence to be written today, rather than the paragraph that I just asked for."

***

"' get out of plane *y mi hermana* she scream."

"Good start, Awilda. Keep it all in English."

"'It rain.'"

"I know it's a sentence, but a little more information, Juan."

"'Y no frogs.'"

"Better, Juan."

The classroom door opened and the dean stepped through. "Professor Hedman, may I see a first draft soon?" The door closed.

Alma stared at the door, turned toward the class, and said, "You aren't the only ones with a writing assignment. Now, who's next?"

"Yo, Teacher, I read."

"Good, Carmelo."

"'It snow. I hear about snow.' *Es two* sentences, Teacher."

"Good. I like the two sentences. Why don't you try for one more? Tell me more about that day."

He wished he could, because it was glued in his brain like the night song of *el coqui* that he will never forget.

Chapter 42

OFFICE OF ACADEMIC AFFAIRS

The Office of Academic Affairs is located on the sixth floor of the warehouse annex *and overlooks a parking lot with barbed wire atop the surrounding wooden fence, which doesn't stop batteries from being stolen out of various professors' cars.* The office includes the president and the provost, as well as the dean of academic affairs, *who informed Carmelo before he registered that there was no course in motor repair, which caused disgruntlement and also a high degree of absenteeism on Carmelo's part. In spite of the distraction of Nurys, Carmelo is beginning to show some interest in learning English, and actually described his first day in this country by writing about snow . . . and perhaps the bruises on his neck indicate a more private visit from this girlfriend, Nurys? This professor knows that can happen in some kinds of lovemaking.*

Chapter 43

"Ah, Professor Hedman. Nice to catch you in your office. Tell me, how is it coming? I thought I would have a first draft by now."

"It's coming along, thank you, Dean Stravronousky."

"And?"

"I'm nearly finished with the introduction, the administrative divisions, and am about to start on the dean of students, student services, and then the faculty. I am waiting for many of their reports."

"I'll send a memo. Hurry them up. Still have some time, but need to meet that first deadline."

"Yes, of course." *Our Lord needs from us neither great deeds nor profound thoughts, just deadlines.*

"I'm sorry. I didn't hear you, Professor Hedman. Were you talking to me?"

"No, no, I don't think so. Just—"

"I'll be looking for that draft."

"Yes, of course."

"Don't really have that much time, now that I think about it, so ..." The dean did not finish his sentence, but turned and went through the office door.

Delores looked up from her desk. "He's a tough one, that dean. Think you can handle that report?"

"I have to." Alma put the student papers down and typed the next heading:

Office of Academic Affairs, cont.

The Office of Academic Affairs is overseer, not only of academic affairs, but, since the president and the provost are part of this division, it is also the fundraising overseer, which of course is the primary concern of the president, while the dean *bursts into the classroom of a professor after hearing her take the roll, stumble to the blackboard, and get interrupted by him in the middle of Juan's sentence about frogs with a drawing of a horse on the blackboard with its rear prominent and a cart precariously attached to some homemade reins, and this is, of course, no way to write a report, but what on earth is all that white clothing about in the middle of winter . . .*

Alma stopped typing and said, "What is all that white about, Delores, that a bunch of students are wearing all the time? Why?"

"They're initiates."

"Into what?"

"They're getting ready to make the saint. Not *your* kind of saint that you mumble about and quote. I don't know what I'm going to do about my son."

"Don't worry about your son. He'll be fine. What do you mean 'make the saint'?"

"Asiento. They'll have their asiento."

"Huh?"

"They become saints. I said not your kind. They acquire power, and they can make things happen."

"Like what?"

"Oh, spells . . . *despojos*."

"What's that, *despojos?*"

"Cleansings, I think, and they can perform *ebbós*."

"What on earth is that?"

"Oh, I don't know. It's not my thing. My uncle was one. But don't get me into it. Something about making your lover more attentive, or whatever it is you want. Like I say, it's not my thing."

"Just curious about all that white stretched across the back row. What do they do once they are a saint?"

"Like I said, they can do stuff, cleanings and the like. Set up *ebbós*. I should call a babalowa and get him to cleanse my son. Not really. Just kidding, but he sure needs a good something. You'd better get back to your report, and I'd better get to class."

What did that saint say? Oh yes, "If her priests are saints, what good they are able to do! But whatever they are, never speak against them." I think it was John Vianney.

Chapter 44

STUDENT SERVICES

The Department of Student Services, headed by the dean of students, coordinates all student service functions and includes a hall monitoring system, which was incorporated after the initial financial crises when halls were being used as classrooms. It was found that, without area designations, however, students were not only interrupting classes in session, but confusing the desks and chairs meant for instruction with desks and chairs for lunch and lounging. *Carmelo and Nurys, in particular, confused the purpose of these areas, and used them for intimate tête-à-têtes.*

A complete range of non-instructional services are available to the students, including vouchers for books, *and Carmelo lost his vouchers and had to pay for his books out of his financial aid money directly, which means that he didn't pay any of what he owed Maria and Mario, which he couldn't do anyway since he had no job yet, and there is some problem with a Rudolfo, and all of which he probably or maybe told Nurys in one of those whispering moments, pieces of which floated to Professor Hedman's ears.*

Chapter 45

"So, hermanito, so now you payin' me rent, huh? Where you get this money? I no give you all dis money, just for food and subway. Where all this come from? What's the job? Where's the job? Who's the boss? What's the pay? When did ya start? *¡Digame, digame!*"

How could he answer any of that?

"Ya not talking? Don't wanna brag, uh? S'okay, pequito hermano, we can take braggin' from you."

"*Qué es* 'brag'?"

"Huh? Waaaaaaait a minute. Look at this kid, Rudolfo. You think maybe he no got a job? You think?"

"I think you're right, man. Don't look like he's happy. Over there with his chin in bed in his hand and his eyes weepin' and staring down at his peepee."

Rudolfo better shut up before he punches him in the gut for real. It's his candy he sold, and he's acting like he knows nothing.

"Bet you new boss ask ya if you knowed English, right? That how you got a job?" Mario grinned.

He should make that finger thing that his fake guardian angel of the subway did. But it might make Mario mad, and he didn't need a mad Mario right now.

"So, dude, here I is, the CEO of a thriving business employing Mario, your brother here, Maria, and two or three others you guys don't know yet, and making good money. Right, Mario?

And I mention this to Mario when you first were coming, and he says, no, his brother is going to school and get an education so he can be a—"

"Shut up, Rudolfo. He'll be coming to that I is sure, but he need to prove hisself in the world and not have it easy handed to him on a silver dish like that, with his never learning nothing 'cause of your big money going down his gullet. So, *shut up!* He better not be working for you."

"Okay, bro. Geez! Geez, geez, geez. I'm just trying to help!"

He didn't need to fight Rudolfo. Mario just did it for him. Mario, his love brother. Mami said he was a good brother. This must be the "little thing" goin' that Mario talked about on the way from the airport that he was supposed to be doing too, so why doesn't he want him doing it now? It would be better than selling this candy.

"*¿Porqué*, Mario? *¿No puede trabajo por* Rudolfo?"

"*Porqué*, you little shit? You not getting your rent money *that* easy. You do a conquering-the-world bit if you ain't going to school, hear me? I give you other mechanic and body places, you try 'em *all* before you work with Rudolfo."

"*¡Sí! Pero*, Mario . . . *yo . . . pero . . . escuela* . . . I goin'."

"Don't you be playin' wid me! 'Member dat. And you no be workin' and learnin' English at the same time."

Chapter 46

This Spanish hubbub seemed to have had something to do with catalogues. Nurys and Awilda were showing them, pointing to pages, and filling in forms, as others pointed and said "*ese, ese.*"

Alma walked to the front of the room. Like the slow closing of a liturgical mass, the hubbub ebbed and some of the catalogues closed and lay flat on the desks.

"Teacher," Nurys waved her catalogue in front of Alma.

"No, Nurys. No."

Nurys put the catalogue down. She folded her hands on her desk and looked at Alma through slitted tiger eyes, and Alma read those eyes and said, "I will order a lipstick from you, but I want you to write a paragraph about why I should wear lipstick, and what color I should wear, and why I should wear that color."

Nurys' eyes opened wide. "That hard, Teacher."

"Do you want extra credit?"

"What extra credit?"

"A better mark."

"Okay. I do it. *Pero* . . ."

Alma watched Nurys put the catalogue in her bag as she took handouts from her own bag. "Today is review. Of questions. Review of information questions words, 'wh' words, plus 'how.' Here are some questions with blanks for you to fill in. The first one is like this . . ."

She wrote on the board: "___ is your name?"

"That one is easy. They get more difficult."

She wrote on the board again. *The handouts flap over her arm like a big bandage*, Carmelo thought, as he watched his teacher look silly.

"I have them written here on these handouts, so in case you don't finish in class, you can take them home. Here is the second question. Fill in the blanks."

"___ content course are you taking in English?"

"___ do you come to school every day?"

She continued writing until ten questions were on the board, and then said, "After you have filled in the blanks, I want you to answer the questions. Allow space after each question for your answer."

She turned away from the blackboard and walked down the aisle. She laid a handout on each desk.

"Is a test, Teacher?" Herman took the handout and pulled a pen from his pocket.

"No, it is not a test, Herman. It is a review." She picked up the next handout, but it clung to the others and would not separate from them.

Nurys rummaged in her bag.

"Write the paragraph, Nurys," she said as she tried to loosen the top sheet from its grip on the next.

"You face, Teacher. You need a blush. You want a buy a blush?"

"No, just the lipstick, Nurys. Begin the paragraph."

"I do. Mira. I begin."

Alma rubbed harder at the corner of the top sheet.

"My teacher she have . . . No, she has . . . She has skin *blanca* . . . *cómo la luna… qué es eso, Luna?*"

"Moon."

"Like la moon."

"You do not need to say it as you write, Nurys." She succeeded in loosening the next sheet and peeled it from the pile. It flew up and clung to her sweater sleeve.

"*¡Dios mío!*" Mercedes, whose desk Alma was next to, stood up and stepped quickly away from her desk, waving her arms. "*La professora es* la Virgin of Midnight."

Alma shook her head. "Mercedes, it's just static electricity." She took the sheet off of her sleeve. It flapped slightly in the air.

"*¡Dios mío!*"

"Mercedes, sit down."

Mercedes sat down.

"The face of mi professor it look . . . it need a blush."

"Please, Nurys." Alma laid the slightly flapping sheet of paper on Mercedes' desk. Her hand and Mercedes' hand met on the desk, an accidental touch. *Ping!*

They both felt the shock, and they and the class heard the small, sharp noise.

"*¡Ella es bruja, bruja!*" yelled Mercedes as she got up and ran to the door. She opened it and went through it, swooshing her skirt against the doorjamb.

"*Estúpido y ignorante.*" Pedro made a gesture toward the door.

"Who would like to go and explain static electricity in Spanish to Mercedes?"

"Yo," said Pedro and stood up.

"Yo," said Jose and stood up.

"One, not both of you." Alma walked toward the two of them. Pedro and Jose looked at each other. Heads in the class turned and looked at Pedro and Jose looking at each other.

"Eenie meenie minie moe . . ." Alma raised her arm to separate Pedro and Jose, who were staring with eagle eyes, and heads all stopped turning toward the two boys and looked at their professor saying "Eenie meenie minie moe," and somebody said in a low quiet voice, "*¡Mira—la bruja, sí!*"

Pedro and Jose said in one voice, "*La professora no es* a witch," and then they laughed at their accidental English chorus, slapped hands, and sat down.

Mercedes came into the room and walked majestically to her desk and sat.

Alma put the remaining pile of paper on an empty desk. "Here they are. Come and take one. *Toma.*"

She stood by the blackboard while bodies moved, arms reached, hands picked and peeled, and small shocks reverberated around the room, and somebody said, "*Todos los estudiantes son brujos and brujas,*" and Alma said, "The next class will be a science lesson."

Let the world indulge its madness, for it cannot endure and passes like a shadow.

"Y earrings. Teacher, why you no use earrings? I give you earrings. *¡Qué linda! Ahora.* Now I write. Mi professor is white skin, short measure. *Es correcto,* Teacher?"

"Has white skin and is short."

Alma saw Carmelo raise his hand. She nodded to him and said, "Yes, Carmelo?"

"Ah . . ." How can he ask her, his teacher nun, why she was buying lipstick from Nurys, who would take her money and put it in her pocket and keep it and never get the lipstick to this nun who probably would never wear it anyway, and . . .

"Yes, Carmelo? You had a question?"

"Ah . . . *porque* . . . ?"

"Why what?"

"No *sé.*"

Alma turned away from Carmelo and looked at Nurys, who was pulling a catalogue from her bag. "Nurys!"

"No, Teacher, I not sell. I find words."

But Carmelo's real question was for Nurys, and it was where and when the money transaction would happen. He didn't want bad news eating holes in his pocket, and he needed to get Rudolfo out of his life.

"Your homework for tomorrow, boys and girls, is to answer the question on the handout. Class dismissed."

Carmelo pulled Rudolfo's bills from his pocket. "Nurys, Nurys!" he yelled, holding up the money, but she ran by him, whispering, "Not here, you stupid," and disappeared.

Chapter 47

STUDENT SERVICES, CONT.

DEAN OF STUDENTS

The assistant to the dean of students/director of student activities reports directly to the dean of students and is responsible for various assignments and projects as designated by the dean. He follows up on projects initiated by the dean, *aside from assisting students like Carmelo with their course schedules, in spite of the fact that these students like Carmelo want what he can't give them, and actually it was the dean himself who set Carmelo's schedule, but this does not indicate a lack of power on the part of the assistant to the dean, who may yet see Carmelo in his office for extensive absences.*

The assistant to the dean of students is a member of the dean's staff and reports directly to the dean of students, substitutes for the dean in his absence, and supervises various projects, *and at least Carmelo isn't wearing white to class when he DOES come, so his obvious outside activity is not becoming a saint, or asiento, or whatever it is.*

***

Alma closed the computer and said to Delores, "Do you want to know what Saint Frances de Sales said about saints?"

"Not really."

"He said that 'All the science of the saints is included in these two things: to do and to suffer. And whoever had done these two things badly, has made himself not saintly.'"

"Thanks for that information, Alma. Don't you have a class?"

"Yes. I'm going now."

Alma pushed Saint Francis de Sales out of her mind, put her roll book in her briefcase, stood up from her desk, and walked to the door, mumbling on the way, "Yes, Saint Francis, I've done and I've suffered . . . badly, so saintly I'm not. But I am a teacher, and what am I doing in class today? Oh yes, the present continuous tense."

But the saint would not leave her and she kept mumbling all the way to the head of the class. "Yes, Saint Francis, I've done and I've suffered badly, so saintly I'm not."

"The present continuous tense, class, which is now, not una momento, *pero* in this moment. Awilda, please stand up. Thank you. Now, say . . . dice . . . 'I am standing here . . . *aqui* . . . here.'"

"Teacher, what you say a youself afore? Then you say '*aqui*.' You speak in Spanish?"

"No, Awilda. No. *Un pequito*." Alma put her thumb and forefinger together, making a "little" sign, and said to Awilda. "*Comprendez?*"

"*Sí.* I am standing here. *Correcto*, Teacher? *Pero* I no stand. I sit."

"Yes, I know, Awilda. But this is pretend. This is practice. This is learning. Repeat after me: 'I am standing, you are standing, he/she is standing, we are standing, you are standing, they are standing.' Repeat this to yourself on the way home after you do the assignment."

"*Bueno*, Teacher. We standing en subway."

"The auxiliary, Juan, the auxiliary. Do not forget the auxiliary. We *are* standing. Now, your assignment is to go after class—after *all* your classes—and find a street corner, sit down with a pad and pencil, and describe what you see in that moment, using the present continuous tense. Remember, use 'is' and 'are,' singular and plural. Or the present continuous tense, 'he is begging' or 'they are yelling.'"

Loco, loco, loco went from student to student.

"Well, yes, maybe it is crazy, but you can explain to the police that you are writing an assignment, and if you stand or sit just outside of the door to the school, I don't think the police will bother you."

"*Pero . . . pero*, Teacher, if we sit by school, a cop . . . the police . . ."

"Then you can include that in your little writing scene perhaps, Jorge."

"This is a difficult assignment, class, but I know you can do it."

Chapter 48

Memo

    To: Mama

    From: Alma

    RE: My Life

I apologize for not responding to your numerous letters. Your last one sounded so desperate that I do now respond.

Please be reassured that my weekends are adequately busy.

Give me your definition of "social life," and then I can answer the question that relates to the term. Perhaps conversing with Delores, my officemate, might come under the category of social life, since we occasionally have coffee together.

I have joined the church, which you bade me to find that day as you stopped the car and delivered me into the heart, or rather bowels, of the big city, and am considering joining the Altar Guild. I help out in the office when I am needed, and play checkers with Father William. I also, of course, read student papers, of which I have over two hundred a week, although I must admit most are rather short.

I am also writing a self-study report for the reaccreditation of the college, which I was assigned to do by the dean. I am currently writing about student services, which are quite adequate. Next is governance. No, faculty. Whatever.

Please also define the verb "seeing" in relation to the pronoun form "anyone," and I then can respond to that reference in your letter. If I am right about your meaning, then let me reiterate that virginity is the highest calling. Remember what Anthony Mary Claret said, Mother, which you said to me, remember? "Doubtless the state of virginity and continence is more perfect." Okay, yes, she said more. There was a "but." However, for now I'm living with the first part of what she said.

Respectfully submitted,

Alma

PS: Also, don't forget that one who governs his passions is master of the world.

Chapter 49

"So here you are! I'm lookin' all over. You not in *our* place. Why you over here? Picking some corner of the park where I no can find you? Never mind. I find now. *Tambien*. Ecoutez."

Just looking for a place to be still and quiet and figure out if he should stay in this college or try another job place, and as soon as he sits here in the quiet, she is . . . but good, she's back talking Spanish to him.

"Ecoutez. I tell my uncle about you having that Blossom Bar, and he say you do better with him in the crack business. He make Zeus Bars. You know, like Mars, only Zeus. Get it? Puts stuff in them so the feds don't see what's really there. Smart, huh? And he says he give me commission, like I already tell you, like a percent if I find him buyers, *pero* when I not see you, I was afraid you not be here, and I need that fifty for him, not half like before. Don't tell me yet. First tell me you be my amor. Put your hand here."

"No, come on Nurys. None of that." *But how could he not pat*
. . .

"Good. Feel good, Carmelo baby? Now give me fifty."

"I no puedo fifty." It did feel good, that nice, soft, round . . . Did that mean he loved her?

"No, wait, I know. Tell you friend you need a hundred mas."

"*¡No es mi amigo!!*"

"Then whoever—and get your hand off of me. If you love me, you do what I say."

He took his hand off of her breast and tried to understand her.

"And do you know what, Carmelo? *Todos los classe escribe en* English now, and speak too, better and better every time, and you *es estúpido, pero* you no even try."

"*Sí, sí, yo* . . . try."

"*¡Mira!* You say 'no *es, mi amigo*' and that not English, and you no even say yes in English, and I need *one hundred*."

Why did Nurys even care if he spoke and wrote in English? She should just leave him be.

Nurys pushed her hand toward Carmelo's pocket and stopped. "Damn."

"*Mañana*," she said as a policeman walked up to them and said, "Get moving."

Chapter 50

"Hey, dude. You Carmelo?"

Was he the dude this man was talking to? Couldn't he finish this essay for his teacher without being interrupted? Even if he couldn't write it in English! "Write it in Spanish," she said, and then she said, "And translate it." Okay, he could try that.

"Hey, dude. You Carmelo?"

He stared at this short dark *abuelo* who was calling him by name. He couldn't be talking to him anyway—some other Carmelo. He was too far away, far away from him, which was way over by that great big square of black velvet cloth with jewelry spread all over it, and now leaning on the table that had the black cloth and jewelry on it, and if he leans any harder, the whole jewelry business will be flat on the sidewalk here in front of his school, or it'll get pushed off the curb into the street. And he's having enough trouble describing the street without getting noticed writing this stupid essay for his crazy—*sí, ella es loco*—teacher saying, "*Escribe* in *el* present continuous tense," which he did not even know what it was in Spanish, and was that dude man turning around now and coming toward him? He should get busy and write so maybe he would be ignored. Write fast—in Spanish he could. "*Medias lunas de oro y de mármel verde jade y un hombre vendiendo naranjas peladas . . .*"

"You deaf or somptin? Or maybe you ain't the dude I want."

That's right, man, keep going.

"Guess you ain't. Since you no answer."

Good. He's gone. Now to translate it. Can't do that. All that description he can't put in English. He'd try. "A man sell . . . is sell . . . selling." And a topic sentence—she said to be sure not to forget the topic sentence. Like maybe I say "In street . . . I stand in el street. No . . . I . . . is. . . ."

Fuck! Back to Spanish. Write. Fast. "*Miro . . . pequeño . . . blanco con cabeza y cascabel pequeño la piel sintetica.*" This is fun, but it's not in English.

"Hi, Carmelo. You doin' that assignment essay thing?"

Ah, Nurys! "*Yo trato.*" She's peering over his shoulder. She shouldn't do that. This is private. Writing is private.

"Let me see what you write. Hey, this no in English, *estúpido.* It no even good Spanish sentences."

"*Yo sé, pero—*"

"*Tambien.* I know. I'll translate it for you if you want, and maybe that'll let you learn English better, and then maybe you be my boyfriend."

Nurys pulled paper from her bag, sat on the sidewalk, and grabbed the pencil from his hand. She looked at his paper and wrote on hers: "I see small . . . things."

"I guess this is what you wrote."

". . . of white fur with heads, and they got sleigh bells tiny."

How can she do that? And so fast? And she should write that they are lying on a green cloth, looking like spilled enchiladas.

"This is all I can do. I gotta go get some jewelry and maybe jeans."

She got up and left him sitting like a wild turkey surrounded by people selling and yelling, and now there comes another truck.

And now that dude *is* walking back toward him and looking at him like a cop, and what's he saying? He's yelling, yelling at *him.* "Her, she's Nurys, mi niece, says you is the one I want."

When did she say that? She's sliding a jade bracelet on her wrist. She's too busy staring at how it's dangling.

"See her? Yeah, her. She say you a good business person."

Stupid Nurys. She looks like she is going to spend money on stupid junk.

"She say you wanna buy some. I her uncle, her tio, so I come to check you out to see if that be true you a good business person."

This guy is talking in English and too fast, and Nurys, she's not just standing now, but leaning herself over that table, too, and brushing against the frayed edges with long threads hanging, and touching gold crescents that look like his Puerto Rican sun, big enough earrings to be real suns hanging from her ears. Now she's putting on a bracelet, then taking it off and moving over to where the small bundles of white fur are wiggling on this green velvet panel.

"She tell you you buy from me? But be quick. We in front of this here school here."

They *would* look good on her, and if only he could write all that describing!

"Come on, bud ... answer me! She say you buy. Be quick!"

"No, *otra* time. *Tambien ... escuela ... ici.* Nurys say—"

"Then Nurys lie! But you buy!"

Carmelo rubbed his two index fingers together and shook his head. "No."

"You motherfucker, I got it and I gotta get it off from me, and Nurys say ... I gotta get out a here with it, so I see *mañana*, and you buy, you motherfucker."

Carmelo stood up and walked away from what was sounding like "fuck fuck fuck" behind him. He walked fast before the fucks turned into more than words. He walked in back of Nurys, seeing her out of the corner of his eye drop the bracelet she had and pick up another one, a gold chain, and slide that over her hand so it dangled and dropped more green light on her little-bit-light-brown arm.

The fucks faded, but he could still be close. "Nurys! Nurys! *Nurys! Ese su tio y . . .*"

He knew it was, but he had to tell her that her uncle was in the wrong place. She was staring at that gold chain, though, and in love with her arm. He turned. The fucks had stopped. Yes, the uncle was gone. Now a small truck was pulling up next to the curb.

"Gotta be three feet. What ya sellin'?"

Is this jewelry salesman talking to him? No, to that other guy in that other truck.

He moved. Back toward his place by the building where the words to his essay came only in Spanish. He squatted against the wall again and opened his pad of paper. He could describe it all in Spanish: the worry, the jealousy, the desire, the greed, the ugly cheap junk, and the orange juice squirting from the peeled oranges that people were eating while walking along in front of the black velvet tablecloth, landing on this sacred mercurial cloth between fake jade and fake gold—but he couldn't do it in English. Nurys did some, but it wasn't full enough for him; there was so much more he needed to say.

The driver of the small truck got out of his truck, opened the side panel door, and pulled out a green velvet square that was making little bell sounds. Who needed bells ringing? Enough was ringing in his ears.

Geez, here was another truck. This truck, though, is bigger, red, like Rudolfo's color, but not him. Can't be. Wait! Who's that getting out of the truck? Some woman. Dragging a table out and setting it up—wiping it—getting a big yellow towel, awful dirty, and spreading it on the table, like Maria saying, makes it pretty, having a table cloth. But why is a woman doing that? Here on the street? Is she going to serve a meal? Now she's leaning into the truck, with her packed-in-tight ass, two-handful-pound of rear-end looking out at the sidewalk, at the college, at him, swaying. What's she getting? What does she have? Okay, a pile of crease-folded jet blue jeans. She's making piles on that long yellow-covered table, lifting some, flapping them back down, running her hand down the sides of the piles and smoothing them. Probably hot! Had to be!

Women showing up now—like chicks to the hens. He knew some of them, picking up, unfolding, holding against their stomachs, kicking their feet beneath, looking down at the kick, making the waist fit their waist, lifting shirts, blouses. And now there is Nurys at this jeans table.

He got up and walked over to her. He wanted an answer from her, even though he knew it had to be her uncle. She was laying a jeans pant leg against her own leg.

"So why didn't you buy from him?" She tossed her head at him and said, "You were supposed to follow him away from the school, dummy. Remember what we talked?"

How was he to know that? She didn't say. "No sabe."

"You could think. You not stupid . . . *estúpido*." She tossed her head again and walked away. To the jeans table, he saw. And there's that driver leaning out the window and yelling, "Ten bucks! Ladies jeans, only ten bucks."

He should yell, "Stolen ladies jeans." Could do it only in Spanish though. They would be in stores if they weren't, not in a truck in the street.

Is Nurys buying? Holy shit, there's his teacher. Looking. She's only looking. That has to be allowed. Only looking. He could see that by the way she waved her hand at the woman suggesting. Only looking. But her hand is on a pile now. No, now it's moving to another pile. And another. Nurys is talking to her.

Holy shit. Nurys is holding up a pair against her, on her. Against *la professora*. Making the waist fit her waist and watching her foot kick out from under the leg. Doesn't Nurys know they have to be hot? Maybe not. He should tell his teacher. It's his duty. Before she gets out her money and sends herself to jail.

He pushed himself away from the wall where he had planted himself, and walked with his pad of paper over past the jewelry and bobbing white fur teddy bears to the table of jeans. He's too late. She is receiving her change and hanging onto a bag.

He put his hand on her shoulder and said anyway, "Teacher." Then he saw the face in the truck window. Rudolfo.

"Rudolfo, fucking Rudolfo!"

"Hi, kid. Meet Ceil. You ain't meet her yet. She's great, don't you think?"

Why is Rudolfo grinning? Why is he so happy?

"You got my stuff?"

Why is he whispering?

"I'm expanding!"

And now he's yelling and leaning out further out of his truck window, getting closer to him and saying again, low, with his teeth tight together, "Do you have it?" Then loud again, "Don't got no men's yet, only ladies. I mean, I'm expanding my territory. Thought to try up here. We only into ladies so far. What are you lookin' at me like that for, kid? Ceil here, she's good. I said, Puffy Face, you got my stuff?"

"No. No, not—"

"You better get it quick, like slick quick, buddy."

Maybe he should have let that uncle . . .

"Ceil here, like I say, she's good. Fast. Today she got off so she could help with the sellin', so you see she's jellin'. See my fist, little bro?"

Fucking Rudolfo!

"Hey, kid, what's the attitude? You bro wouldn't like that attitude with his Rudolfo, so ya better cut it out. Hey, don't start nothin' here. You embarrass you school. You don't wanna do that now, do ya? Get away from that table. Come on, you won't make your brother proud that way. This here is your school you gonna embarrass, so cut it out. Hey, what the fuck!"

Carmelo heard the screams and saw his arm clear the table, and saw the yellow towel fly into the boulevard and land on top of a black limousine, and saw jeans in heaps fly off the table and Ceil jumping down the sidewalk trying to catch them. He saw Rudolfo come across the table, and then he felt his head splash somewhere, and small bundles of white fur with white fur heads, arms, and legs wiggled on little sleigh bells on a green cloth, spilled enchiladas *Y ahora es una muchacha* sliding a jade bracelet dangling green on a light-brown arm. Nurys. And Teacher Alma looking down on him like a Madonna?

Chapter 51

He woke up. A white dress—a saint?—and a hand with a thermometer in it. And white walls and Maria crying. And Mario! Where was Rudolfo? He was not finished. He still needed to smash his face.

Is that Mario he's hearing? "You are goin' home. As soon as you get outta this hospital, you is going back to Mami. I got your ticket right here. You is clearin' outta here and clearin' outta this city and outta my life."

He turned his head and closed his eyes. He couldn't clear out. He had to write that present continuous tense thing and give it to Professor Hedman in her goddamn hot blue jeans.

"¡*TONTO!* You *tonto!*"

Was that Mario?

"*Yo no estúpido*, Mario."

"Yeah, you stupid, and the mushroom woman's gonna put boils up your ass."

"No, Mario, no *estúpido, pero* Rudolfo, *el es . . . el malo.*"

"Don't you be blamin' Rudolfo."

"*Y ojalateria . . .*" He needs to be that.

"Yeah, a stupid tin man. Ya gotta be smart to be a body shop people, and if you get kicked outta school, forget it."

"No, Mario, that not happen . . . *ojalateria* . . . a collision man, *pero* Rudolfo *es—*"

130

"But you outta here and back to Mami anyway, so forget it for that too."

"No, Mario, no. I be a collision man *y no malo hasta la médula cómo* Rudolfo! He be sellin'—"

"Go the fuck to sleep, and when you wake up you has you ticket—"

"Drugs," but his words went into the white white wall, and other words went into his head: *You my sweet, kind boy. New York City is not a kind, sweet city. Be careful. Do not get into fights. Keep your kind, sweet self.*

And now he has to tell Mami he is no kind, sweet boy. And this not-kind-sweet city is swallowing his whole life like a rat-eating *el coqui*.

Chapter 52

He can't go back. He has to bring money to Mami when he goes back. And he needs English to get the money.

"You is one lucky Latin idiot, bro. Rudolfo done defend you to the police, or you be in the slammer right now."

Rudolfo defended him? Why? Rudolfo needed to defend himself.

"What was in you fucking head you attack, *mi amigo con todo*?"

Mario did not know what he knew. He did not know because he wouldn't listen to him. Let him talk to the wall. So how should he tell him so he would listen? The stealing Mario knew about, and did himself, but not the other, not the crack dealing. So stealing was nothing to Mario. Stealing is no big deal. But the other? He would never go for *that*!

"So okay, what's with that Nurys? You new girlfriend? What's with Miguelina? Can't you even be true? And that professora? Who she to you? You is way too much for me to handle. Go home to Mama, you fucking bro!"

"Mario! *¡Escucha!*"

"I ain't listenin' to nothin.'"

"You listen to a *mi*. You *amigo es*—"

"I *said* I ain't listenin'—especial nothin' bout *mi amigo*."

"Fuck! And I no go a *mi casa*—"

132

"*Tambien*, you stay, you pay rent every week, not just when you feels like it! And you no wait for that bandage be off you idiot head either."

Chapter 53

Alma walked into the classroom mumbling to a saint, and looked at Juan writing on the blackboard. "The Classe *es* United Nations."

She walked to the back of the room and leaned against the wall. She watched him point to Angelica, who said, "El Salvador." He pointed to Norman, who said, "Nicaragua." He pointed to himself and said, "PR."

"You forget me, Ecuador," said Jorge.

"You forget Carmelo," said Nurys, and Juan put his finger under his chin and pushed it up and said, "He no here."

"He in la clase."

"Yeah, *pero no es aquí ahora.*"

Why was she letting this happen? Of course, it gave her more time to feel Carmelo's head in her lap and wonder if he would ever come back to school. But teach she must.

She stood away from the wall. "Say it in English, Juan." It would be good practice for Juan to lead the class—that would be teaching too.

The light from the window threw golden darts on the blackboard. Probably a sign. It lit the small window in the classroom door, she noticed, until a shadow took its place there. She turned her head toward this now moving shadow, which was making slow movements over a white bandage and a sad smile.

***

Everybody could probably see him through this window, since he could see in—even if this window was tiny. So what was the matter with him coming to school like this, with this big white bandage still on his head making him look like a Santeria *chiflada,* a crazy saint, or something.

And Nurys was probably staring at him like an orisha or something, and what is Juan doing in front of the class pointing at everyone alone, like a cop saying 'you and you and you and you,' and why is the teacher in the back of the room watching him do this and not doing her job? Uh oh, did she just turn her head and see him? Sooner or later he would have to go in. He was here, and was sure not going home to Maria and Mario.

He opened the door. Nurys' voice? Yes.

"Like I say, you forget Carmelo, Juan." Maybe she wasn't mad at him.

"*Sí,* Teacher. Like I say, he not here."

What was Juan's problem? He was right here. Juan was fucking blind.

"Say it correctly, Juan, please, with a verb."

And the teacher too? Was she blind?

"Carmelo is not here now." Was that Juan? Sounding gleeful?

So he was invisible. Maybe that light coming in the window like flittering yellow finches was making everybody blind.

"You did a fine job, Juan. Now, I, as your real teacher, shall take over." Alma stood away from the wall and walked to the front of the class.

"*Qué es* 'take over,' Teacher?"

"It means, Awilda, . . . it means . . . Oh, Carmelo, you *are* here! Please sit down."

Finally. "*¿Dónde?*" There were no empty chairs. Couldn't she see that?

"Oh. Well. Yes. If you would come to class more often, there would be a chair for you. Why don't you stand by the door for now, while I get the class started."

"*¿Aquí? ¿Para la puerta?*" Wasn't he going to be allowed to sit?

"Yes, please just stand there for now. In fact, if you stand there, you can help us start the class. It will be about comparison. Juan, you stand, please, next to Carmelo."

Juan stand next to him? Why? *He* had a chair. And did he have to grin like that and come at him like a Puerto Rican racer, his hoodie turning him into a cobra?

"Juan, do not touch Carmelo, but stand still, quietly—*con silencio*. That's it. Now, class, who is shorter, Carmelo or Juan?"

Juan better take that grin off his face. This was not funny.

"*Qué es* 'short,' Teacher?"

"Like this . . ."

Carmelo watched his teacher move one hand above her head and say "tall" and laid the other flat in the air below her waist and say "short." And Juan slapped his chest and said, "I short than Carmelo."

"Good, Juan. You are short*er* than Carmelo. Thank you. Class repeat: 'Juan is shorter than Carmelo.'"

Carmelo knew enough English to know that Juan would not be happy. And if Juan did too, he would not be grinning. And the chorus in the room sounding like frogs was making Juan grin even more. Maybe he liked being short, and he, Carmelo, was the odd one.

"You may sit down, Juan."

What about him, standing by the door like a palm tree?

"And, Carmelo? Oh, yes! Sorry! Go to the next room and bring a chair from there. It's empty. The room, I mean."

Finally, she sees him. Get a chair is what she said. From? "*Dónde?*"

"In the room next to us. In the room . . ." Okay, she's pointing. He can understand that. He could do that. A chair in the room where she's pointing. He would bring two chairs, one for himself and one for his guardian angel, just in case it showed up. He might need it to get rid of Rudolfo.

"Now, class, we are talking about comparison. Ana and Awilda, will you stand, please?"

This teacher is going to do the same thing with those two? He went through the door wondering what difference it made who was shorter.

He walked out of the room and bumped into a chair sitting like a lone *el coqui,* waiting for a chance to give luck to him—like getting Rodolfo from his life—and walked back into the room, put the chair down, and sat on it. He was not close to Nurys, but he was close enough to mouth the words, "*Tango moola,*" not knowing exactly why he was going to tell Nurys that he had money because he was so confused now who was supposed to get money from him and who wasn't, and he did need that his percent from whom—oh *dios.* What? What? What was he supposed to do anyway without getting killed by Rodolfo.

Nurys s shook her head and mouthed, "Shut up. Not here, *estúpido.*"

"Carmelo and Nurys, don't test me."

Does she have to give him *oyes* like that?

"Class, who is tall*er*, Awilda or Ana?"

"Ana!"

"Yes, repeat after me: 'Ana is taller *than* Awilda.'"

"Ana is taller than Awilda."

Now the whole class has gone, *chiflado.*

"By the way, Carmelo, can you tell me who is taller, Awilda or Ana?"

"*¿Cómo?*"

"Hey, Teacher, Carmelo with that bandana on his head, he tall*er* than anybody here!"

"Good, Juan."

Should he get Juan now, or wait 'til after class?

"*¡Mira! ¡Mira!* Teacher, *Mira!*"

Nurys? Now it's Nurys waving her arm and yelling, and now she's reaching way over to him and laying her arm smack up against his arm. "*¡Mira! Mi* . . . my arm *es* . . . is light than Carmelo's arm. See, Teacher?"

"Yes, I see, Nurys. Say 'light*er* than.'"

"*Sí.* Light*er* than."

"*Fuck!*" He swung his arm in the air and stood up. He couldn't hit Nurys, but where was that Juan? He started this. His elbow bent and his arm shot up. His hand made itself into a fist. *Okay, Juan!*

"Wanna fight, Carmelo? Look like you want to? I musta offend you, bro. Is okay. I can take it, bro. You may be taller, but I—"

"*Sí*, Juan. I fight."

"*Yo* think I'm sellin' hot stuff, *muy muy* hot! Search me. I right here."

"You *habla chico* . . ." Carmelo shot his fist out toward Juan and then saw the teacher take small lizard slides through the desks toward him, and then his cheek got hit.

He swung back.

How did he know the teacher was right there and that his fist would punch *her* shoulder and push *her* onto Juan's chest?

The room got quiet.

Then the quiet changed to gasps.

***

"What I got here?" Mario waved a piece of paper at him. "I see this here fallin' outta you bookbag what says on it 'To Guard-I-an of Carmelo,' and I suspectin' that be me, huh? You gonna give it to me or what, huh?"

"*Me olvido.*"

"You forget? This ain't no love letter from you teacher. This here a . . . what the fuck did you do? Hit her?"

"No, no. Juan. *Yo* Juan . . . *la professora sé metio de—*"

"She got in the way? You is a crazy shit. She say here you need . . . help? Therapy? What that? You gotta opologize to that teacher. She say if you don't do sompin' you is sus-pen-dead. You is dead all right. Whatever the hell she say here, it ain't good I gotta feelin'. *Tambien.* You no belong in school, *pero* if you is stayin', you got one more chance with me, *and* like I say, you pay me rent more than what you is now, since you ain't seem to be goin' home. *¡Mira!* I still got you ticket."

Chapter 54

Memo

To: Luis Stravronousky, Dean of Faculty

From: Prof. Alma Hedman, English Department

RE: Incident of October 10

This is in reference to the incident of October 10, which occurred on the sidewalk in front of the college at 11:45 a.m. and involved one Cardenas student, one Cardenas staff member, one Cardenas professor, one blue jean entrepreneur, and one salesperson and his assistant, a woman.

In defense of the professor (myself), this professor had never received the heretofore spoken of (by the dean, in the hall, at 2:00 p.m. on October 10) Policy Guidelines for Conduct of Administrative and Professional Personnel Concerning Street Vendors, and thus did not know of said policies.

This professor (myself) apologizes for the purchase and has since donated same to the Christmas toy and clothing fund being sponsored by the Math and English Department Learning Lab.

Also, in defense of the involved student, Carmelo Rodriguez, there must have been a legitimate reason for this young man's admittedly volatile action. I will attempt to discern what it was at the earliest opportunity. He has been my student for the past two semesters, and although irregular in performance and attendance, is motivated and sincere in his work. The fact that the incident erupted at the moment that the ex-officio vice-chancellor of the university and university dean of Interracial Affairs and the president of the Board of Higher Education were stepping from their limousine and preparing to enter the college was unfortunate. This incident, however, has one positive outcome, in that no street vendors will be hitherto allowed on streets adjacent to the college.

As for any connection between my purchase and Carmelo's action, I am sure there was none. Its coincidental occurrence was a coincidence, I am sure. There is no, and I repeat, no fraternization between said student and myself, as you most tactfully insinuated in the hall on October 10.

I am assuming that your statement was made in haste and in anxiety for the appearance of the college in the eyes of the university administration.

Thank you for your personal as well as professional concern for my tenure here at Cardenas.

**

Memo

To: Professor Alma Hedman

From: Dean Luis Stravronousky

RE: Incident of October 10

Thank you for your candid and thoughtful response to our conversation in the hall on October 10 at 2:00 p.m. suggesting that you peruse the Guidelines for Conduct of Administrative and Professional Personnel Concerning Street Vendors. These guidelines were distributed at the stated faculty meeting at the start of the semester, and were, I believe, announced to be on the table to the right of the coffee and orange juice. However, I can understand an inadvertent overlooking of announced policy changes in the wake of the president's announcement of such drastic budget cuts. Nevertheless, in spite of these more urgent claims on our emotional resources, we must endeavor to "put attention," as our students say, to matters of policy concerning decorum and image of Cardenias Community College.

As for the student in question, who, in an unfortunate manner, precipitated the discovery of the breach of policy, no disciplinary action will be taken at this time, since, as you pointed out earlier, this is his first offense. Therefore, the disciplinary action currently in occurrence, that of a mandatory anger management class, shall be all that is required of him at this time.

In addition, I regret that you read into what I said as an insinuation that fraternization was occurring between you and the student. I am sure that this was a heated response in the moment, as you suggest, to what appeared to me to be an obvious juxtaposition of events that morning. Now, with a cooler head, I see that the two events could be separate. The incident had, more probably, to do with a triangle situation concerning himself, the "entrepreneur" (as you politely call him), and the young woman selling merchandise (which, as we all know, had to be of an illegal source).

At this point, I exonerate all concerned, have written a letter of apology to the ex-officio vice-chancellor, the university dean of Interracial Affairs, and the president of the board. I have also spoken to all of them on the telephone, and they all have assured me that the incident is behind the school and is being attributed merely to the high spirits of youth. They did not mention the professor who was holding the head of the student in question in her lap.

Chapter 55

THE COLLEGE SENATE

The College Senate, under the auspices of the Department of Student Services, operates according to the guidelines and policies of the governance charter and meets once a month to consider matters, *such as rude memos to the deans and rude memos from the deans to the faculty.*

The Senate committees meet according to schedule, and the disciplinary committee meets when called and considers matters of student behavior that have been brought to the Senate's attention, *and Carmelo knows he will one day be before that body if he does not attend the suggested angry management—his phraseology—seminar. The reason for this suggestion on the part of Professor Hedman is an incident whereby she, Professor Hedman, after reciting the stations of the cross to herself as a means of calming an untenable situation, took small kangaroo leaps over to the young men who were in confrontation, ducking under arms that were beginning to swing, and stood up face-to-face with Juan, and received, as a result, a punch on her right shoulder that pushed her face into Juan's face, and she tasted salt, which caused humiliating gasps behind her in the classroom.*

Chapter 56

"Teacher? I have . . . *disculpar*." Carmelo sat down next to his teacher's desk.

"Are you trying to say that you are sorry?"

"*Sí*. Sorry."

"I accept your apology. I would say that some others were the provocateurs, perhaps, but you do have a quick fuse. That is, you use your arms before you talk. Your fuse certainly came into play last week on the street, also. What happened that day to cause the display? You do know that a man who governs his passion is master of the world, don't you?"

"*¿Eh?*"

"Never mind. Tell me what happened on the street that day."

Carmelo decided she was talking about Rudolfo in that truck. "On the street, Teacher?"

"Yes, on the street."

"*Es muy difícil dar explicaciones o de entender.*"

"I'm sure it is hard to explain, but try, in English, anyway."

"*Ayer* no . . .*un otra dia Rudolfo en la truck.*"

"Yes, and you disrupted the clothing table." *And hit your head on the sidewalk when you were hit by that man, and I held your head in my lap.*

"*Sí*, *sí*. That . . . Rudolfo en la truck."

"You knew the vendor, then?"

"*Sí*."

"And the woman was your girlfriend?"

"No, no, Teacher. *Miguelina es mi amor.* She *en* Barranquitas."

"Oh. Then I don't understand all the fuss."

"Rudolfo, he *malo . . . malo.*"

"I can't help you with Rudolfo, but you did have a homework assignment that day. I believe—"

"*Sí. Escribo.* I write."

"Good. For the present continuous tense, right? A description of a sidewalk event, right?"

"*Yo escribo ese.*"

"Good, Good. May I see it, then?"

"*Es en Español. Y por la esplicacion de la . . . de la incidente?*"

"Yes, incident, that's the word. Did you describe what happened on the street? The altercation between you and . . . and a gentleman?"

"Rudolfo, *sí.*"

"That would be complicated for you to write, I would think. Especially since you were taking part in it, I believe, which meant you could hardly be sitting there and describing it."

"*Sí. Pero otra . . .* before . . . *ese yo escribo. Pero no escribo ese. Yo escribo* tables . . the cheap . . . the things."

"May I see that?"

"*Es en Español.* Nurys *trans un pequito.*"

"No, I want to see it in English, and not what Nurys translated for you. So, anyway, you owe me homework. The description for the present continuous tense, plus a comparison, and writing it in Spanish does not count, unless you, and I mean *you*, not your brother or girlfriend, translate it."

"I 'splain. *Pero mi hermano dice* 'get out and go home. Fuck off.' *Pero* I stay. *Trabajo. Y—*"

"Good. And stay in school too."

"*Sí.*"

"And do the homework."

"*Sí.*"

"Rudolfo, he drug traffacaner. *Cómo yo* . . . I say, he—"

"Carmelo, you pay attention to Carmelo. And while you were not in school, we learned the present perfect, so that's a third . . ."

"He put hex. Rudolfo, he . . ."

"the present perfect, and I'll explain that to you now, as long as you are here and I have your attention. Just think of it as the time before the present, that is, since the past comes to meet the present, and may go on to the future, or may not, depending upon whether it's the immediate past or a continuum—"

"*¡Dios mío!*"

"It is not that difficult."

"*¡Dios mío!*"

"I will draw you a time diagram. Look. Here is a point in the past. Are you listening to me? Say, when you came to New York. What year was it? 1993? Around then, right? I'll put 2004 here. That point, that pencil dot, is 1994."

"He *vente a la* Spirit Center."

"And this point is today, now, 1995. Okay?"

"Okay. *Pero* he *vente y* maybe in *closo no mate*—I mean kill me, and Mario no believe me *qué* Rudolfo *es malo.*"

"Now from here to here, or now, is the present time, and you use the auxiliary and past participle to express that time."

"Okay."

"Do you understand that?"

"Okay. ¿Rudolfo *dice a mi qué?* 'I grow a nest of hairy spiders in my heart.' *El dice* a Maria to ask for her madrina to go to a santero and maybe even a babalohoa."

"Look at all that English you just spoke. That's wonderful!"

"*Qué*, teacher? Miguelina, too, say I maybe if no come home *y* she make a hex on me. Rudolfo—"

"And all that English too. Very, very good."

"*Qué*, teacher? No *es bueno*. She make a hex. Rudolfo—"

"Don't be silly. That's all nonsense—hexes are nonsense."

"*Qué es* nonsense?"

"Hexes and hairy spiders and santeros, that's all superstition."

"*Pero, qué es* 'superstition'?"

"Something that isn't true, like hexes and the hairy spider and all that."

"No, you no understand. That is truth. Rudolfo say—"

"Don't worry, Carmelo. Just learn English and don't worry."

"*El es amigo de Mario . . . y Mario es mi hermano.*"

"I know. You told me. I see your quandary. Now, look at this diagram. See the point in the past?"

Carmelo looked down at the paper, at the lines and points and small arrows the teacher drew, and all those lines and her talking about time. It all blurred into lots of points and wavy lines and damp, wet arrows that pointed to goat cheese and spider nests in Miguelina's hair, and hairy lizards, and he groped for Miguelina.

"Do you see? That space in between? That's the time for which you have to learn the words to use. That's the crucial time. Are you listening?"

No, but he should nod anyway.

He nodded. It was amazing how much English the teacher could say at one time. And how much he couldn't. And it was amazing how much the teacher did not understand about his problem.

Chapter 57

ASSISTANT DEAN OF STUDENTS

The assistant dean of students coordinates most student service functions and sees to it that a complete range of non-instructional services are available to the students, including classes in study skills, library instruction, and a new addition to services, that of anger control *which, it has been suggested to Carmelo he take advantage of, even though, as he expressed, his brother is a poor role model, to which this professor suggested that he be a role model for his brother and also that he consider living somewhere else, but financially that seems to not be an option.*

The new addition to the functioning of the Student Services Department mentioned above, that of anger control, has been instituted as a result of unfortunate interchanges on the boulevard between street vendors (since outlawed), some students, and some faculty. Not only did the above-mentioned incident cause the outlawing of the presence of vendors, but a complete rewording of the Guidelines for Conduct of Administration and Professional Personal Concerning Street Vendors. These, for obvious reasons, have been revised, if not expunged at this point due to irrelevancy.

Chapter 58

"You want you read my composition, Carmelo?"

Read Nurys's essay? Why?

"And my uncle say not enough money. What I give him for you that you refuse to give to him youself. And you need a hundred more. Tell your amigo."

"*He no es mi amigo y . . . I no puedo pregunto por mas.*"

"Whatever he is, whoever he is, you have to ask for more. And, hey, I'm talking in English, and so can you. I'm even writing in it. Here, read my composition."

She should not wave it in his face like a dead palm leaf.

"*Read it!*"

"Okay. *Pero es tarde* . . . late."

"After class, then. Come on."

They crossed the street, walked the two blocks, and got in the scanning line in front of the college. Nurys waved her page in front of him again, for long enough that words floated in front of him like bugs. How could he read all those English words? And this scanning? Scanning was ridiculous anyway. There were loads of ways a guy could get a gun or anything else into this building. Besides, isn't this against the law or something? In this free free country? In Barranquitas they did not do this, and guys had guns there. Well, not many. And what about the crack that Nurys is getting for him, for Rudolfo—

that doesn't get picked up by scanning. Or even blossom bars in pockets.

***

"Okay, now read."

They stood in the hall outside their classroom, and Carmelo took the paper from Nurys.

"Out loud!"

"*Es deficil. Pero* 'I never will forget *mi*—'"

"'My,' stupid."

"'*My* child . . . hood? Hood *en mi*—'"

"'In my.' Can't you read?"

"'Town *pequito*.'"

"You shoulda said 'tiny.'"

"'Town in my country *con* mangoes *y* papayas on the trees and in the ground *con* my friends.'"

How was he going to tell Rudolfo he needed a hundred more? "*Mira. Bueno.*"

"You no read it all."

"*Sí.* 'Our favor play was gallanta cobrada. Our favor play next was Dona Ana. To play that we had formed a circle around her . . .'"

Like Miguelina, the one in the center, her long hair twirling around her neck and her long legs making her tall. Standing in the center like that, her arms out like angel wings, her smile sweet and kind.

"Are you reading it or dreamin' on it? But we better get to class now. You can read it there."

Nurys pushed him into the hall wall and whispered into his ear. "I'll meet you tomorrow again in the park, and I'll take half the extra hundred and you can give me the other half next week.

That way you won't have to ask for the extra one hundred right all at once. And you'll meet my uncle again, and *don't* him ignore like before, 'cause he getting mad and he go after you *and* your *amigo*. You were supposed to follow him away from the school, dummy! Remember?"

How was he to know that? "*No sabe.*"

"You could think. You not stupid. To follow him."

Rudolfo would slap him around again and tell him he was lying and that he wanted it for himself.

"So *read*, and say to me what you think about the end of mi composition? Did you like it when I say that when Dona Ana doesn't answer their question it means she is died? And is that okay about tomorrow and the fifty?"

Why was she whispering that last sentence? Oh, because there is a teacher coming down the hall. "You write that? *Pero yo sabe ese* game. *Pero I jamas sabe con ese* ending."

"That *is* the end."

"No, dead is no the end. Miguelina *este* Dona Ana *y* Miguelina never die."

"Who's that? Who's Miguelina? She *en* this here *escuela?*"

"No, no, no, Nurys. She *en* PR."

"Oh! Keep her there."

"No *sé* 'keep her there.'"

"Learn English and you will know what it means. See you in the park tomorrow."

"*Sí. Pero . . .*"

His sentence did not get finished; it did not reach even her back.

Chapter 59

ADDRESSED IMPROVEMENTS

The first self-study report listed three major areas where improvement was imperative. These have been identified, and it is now with pride and self-confidence that we are able to say that improvement has occurred in all three areas: administrative structure, *Nurys and Carmelo seem to be cultivating a close companionship, although minor disruptions sometimes happen, both in and out of the classroom, some of which, this professor has noted have to do with an exchange of small amounts of money,* a new programmatic-module instructional system with accessible computer instruction, mostly in the form of games, which is available on a first-come basis in the Tutoring Center, as well as improvements in maintenance and facilities. As for the latter, the model in the lobby of the proposed way-in-the-future master campus now has a crack in its glass top *from where Carmelo's elbow came down hard on it because of the appearance, evidently, on the sidewalk in front of the building of a young man whom he referred loudly to as "Bro!"*

Chapter 60

Another letter from Mama? No, a letter from Father William. How unusual. Was she being evicted? Her rent not enough?

Alma walked back to her office reading:

Dear Alma,

The deacons have decided against appointing you to the Altar Guild. Do not take this personally, but it was felt that your attendance at worship has been too erratic. You seem less committed of late, and I, of course, understand this—it frequently happens in time of transition. Our doubts often surface after—at any rate, the leap of faith sometimes becomes a bit threadbare. Sometimes it is more of a hobble, shall we say? Are you very disappointed? Please do come by for a game of checkers when you are not, as you say, "inundated" with papers.

PS. But if you have any old linen, the Guild ladies asked me to ask you, they are low on purification cloths.

She'd never use all that linen. Her hope chest was totally pointless. So why do you bother adding to it?

"I should have told Mother to forget about that hope chest."

"What did you say, Alma?" Delores pushed her chair back and stood up. "I'm off to class, but is there a problem? You look distraught."

"No, no. Virginity is the highest calling, isn't it, Delores? You're Catholic, and isn't that just like us? Episcopalians, or at least the nuns, believe that."

"You kidding? Maybe I guess if you're a nun, but . . . I'm off to class."

"And I've been fired from the Altar Guild."

"If that were I, I'd be happy. Bye."

"Bye." Alma folded the letter and put it in her bag. One more daily punctuation.

Chapter 61

"What? You want a hundred more? You little shit. This for you? You gonna keep it for youself, you fucker you?"

"No, no, Rudolfo. Nurys say—"

"I believe you that you ain't wanting it for youself. I believe youse, 'cause you have that baby look about you that you bro say is gonna get you in trouble, says you should be toughened up. So's I is taking that upon myself to do. Youse is too soft for this here world. You dress is soft, like you need gold teeth caps and tattoos maybe. You let me, I'll get you fixed up. 'Til then, I ain't giving you a hundred, or even fifty. You can take twenty more and tell your fuckin' Nurys friend that it only because she bought my jeans that day, and it be a wonder she got 'em bought before you goddamn whacked them all down the street. Yeah, I figured out who is she."

He doesn't need a guardian angel. He needs a *curandera*, somebody to get him out of this mess.

"Now get the hell outta my sight."

Yes, he would do that. And get himself in the sight of Nurys, like he was supposed to be seeing her and try to explain why it was only twenty more and not a hundred.

He went down the subway steps into the darkness thinking about his wide Puerto Rican sky.

Chapter 62

Mami said in the airport, "You need a saint with you." She was right, especially now with Nurys saying she wants to be his girlfriend, his amor, which was why she wanted to meet him in the park all the time, not to take the goddamn money and get the goddamn crack. Yes, he touched her bosom. And yes, she made him the first time. And that second time it was an accident. He said that it was an accident, but she did not believe that, and she grabbed his hand and pushed it up her blouse, brushing her belly on the way, and he got a surge.

So if he got a surge, did that mean he loved her?

Carmelo worried about this as he walked to the subway as much as he was worried about the money still stashed in his pocket, which she wouldn't even take, 'cause she said it was for her uncle to take and it wasn't enough anyway. If he did not get rid of it soon, he would be a dead man walking, from giving off vibes that he had money in his pocket. And was Rudolfo even going to accept one-half for the money?

He needed a *curandero*, not a saint. But how was he going to get one? He could do the *ebbós* himself. He could take the bus over to the river and float them, and with the nickel . . .

But maybe it was Oshun he should call for: "*Illa mi ile oro.*" Like that time with Miguelina sitting cross-legged and mixing cinnamon and honey, and she had her other hand on his leg. "This is for our love," she said, and made her fingers dance on his

knee. "*Illa mi ile oro illa mi ile oro vira ye yeye oyo vira ye yeye oro.*"
She sang it. It was magic music from heaven. "*Ya mala ya mala,*"
she ended it and they sat quietly.

That cinnamon and honey was for love, not for getting out
of a drug deal.

Carmelo climbed up the steps to Mario's closed-door
apartment. He opened the door and walked in. Mario was
watching television and had a beer in his hand. He turned and
looked at Carmelo with small bat eyes.

"I don't see no dis month rent, one month only all right." He
pulled an envelope from his pocket. "Here's you ticket. Like I say,
you can get out. You ain't payin' 'nuff rent, and you ain't goin' to
school, and you—"

"No, no, Mario. *En la escuela ahora.*"

"What about yesterday? What about tomorrow?"

"*Sí, sí, mañana, sí.*" He should tell him about the money in
his pocket and what it was for. Let it be *his* problem, and then he
would free, free, *y no malo*, and that percentage could be for this
rent money. And then he could learn English and go back to the
man at the garage and work there after school to get the money
to go back and marry his Miguelina and tell her she can stop
singing at El Caribe, and have the babies, and watch the babies
play Dona Ana and . . .

"Okay. *Mañana* I come to you school, hear?"

"*No!* No, Mario." Mario would never do that. *¡Jamas!*

Chapter 63

¡Dios mío! He did that. There he is. How did he get through with all that metal on him—earrings and belt buckle and bracelets that jangled when he had come through the door that day and had made Maria wince.

"¿Mario, *qué hacer en mi escuela?*" he said to his crazy brother who was standing like a spare tire just inside the revolving door. Yes, he had spied him on the sidewalk outside last week, but didn't think he was ever going to do this. He just thought he was casing for Rudolfo how he could set up a jean table, but now here he was inside his school.

Carmelo pushed through his classmates crowded in the lobby waiting for class and called again to his brother, "¡Mario, *aquí!* What you do *en mi escuela?*" He would have to figure out how to get him out of here.

Mario saw him and waded with his arms through the crowd, got close, and embraced him. "¡*Ahhhhhh, mi hermano!* I come like I say to. Just makin' sure you is where you says you is, and not *arriba en el roofo* doing crack, 'cause Rudolfo say you maybe is gettin' into sompin' to earn money, and I say 'what is that?', and he say he not telling. So, if you is doin' sompin' *malo, malo,* you is using that ticket."

Carmelo's insides shuddered. "No *confías en* me?"

"Sure I trust you. Just checkin' on my own trustin' ya. Rudolfo don't lie to me, but I believe you 'cause you *es mi hermano.* No, I is goin' to see you *maestra.*"

"*¿Qué? ¿Porque?*"

"I have sompin' a say to her."

"You no allow *en la escuela cóme este*. You show you ID?"

"*Sí*. And I gots the permission. See?" Mario waved a paper in front of Carmelo. It did not look official, but Carmelo let it go. "And I's here and I's goin' see you *maestra*. Meet her."

How was he going to keep Mario from climbing the stairs with him and walking down the hall with him and people gawking at big, big Mario walking like a bear and jangling bracelets and going into the classroom? How? He couldn't.

Introduce him. He had to do that. But wait! Maybe this was good. Maybe make him important, to have a big brother. "*¿Quieres conocer a mi professora?*"

"Yeah. That why I come." Mario started up the stairs and Carmelo grabbed his arm.

"No, no, that be *baja*. We go *alta* . . . up." He steered his brother to different stairs. He could not stop him, so he might as well go up the right stairs. They started up together. Was that a tinge of pride he was feeling? Like when Mama came to school in the first grade to meet his teacher?

He looked at Mario lumbering beside him on the stairs. Serious. "How's Maria?" he said, suddenly feeling overwhelming love for his family.

"You see her this morning. Two hours ago. She was fine. Whatsa matter wid you?"

"*Nada, nada.*"

They reached the top of the stairs, and Carmelo walked tall and proud, leading his shining star of Puerto Rican, his brother, into his classroom.

***

"Ola, Teacher! *Este es mi hermano, Mario.*"

"Say that in English, Carmelo."

Mario grinned. "Ha ha! This be a good teacher."

"Carmelo? In English."

"*Sí.* This *es* . . . is my . . . brother, Mario."

"Good. How do you do, Mario? I am pleased to meet you."

"Hallo. Nice meetin' you too. I's just makin sure *mi hermano* here is where he s'pose to be and not *en el roofo* doin' crack."

What the fuck? "*¡Mario!*"

"Anoder thing. I don't want Carmelo here to be doin' no chicken dance between Spanish and English. He's startin' to do that. I want him saying it right, like you, *Professora.*"

"We're doing our best, Mario. You might, however, remind him to be more cognizant of the time class starts and more consistent in his attendance and in doing his work."

Fuck! Did she have to say that to Mario?

Mario was not answering her. He was looking at him, with eyes boring into him like Maria's did, and now walking close to him and saying into his ear, "*Yo no sé this here cognizante, pero* . . . but *you do you fuckin' work* like the teacher say, or I pull you hairs out one by one . . ."

"Now, now, that's all right. Carmelo will be doing fine, Mario."

"*and you is a dead turkey!*"

"Class is about to begin. Would you like to join us Mario? You may sit in on the class."

"*'Cause* if you don't, you is workin' the jeans with Rudolfo and me. Nice meetin' you, Professora. *Mi oyes, mi hermano.* Ola, Professora. *Gracias* por the time you giving me."

¡Dios! He's gone.

"Sit down, Carmelo."

The teacher's glad he's gone too, Carmelo thought, as he sat down and tried to find that love for his family he'd had before.

160

Teacher Alma's back at the blackboard now, and that means she's forgotten what just happened. Maybe he can forget what happened too, if he puts a new idea in his head. Except that he really does not have a new idea.

Alma looked at Carmelo sitting, slumped, his hands holding his head low on the desk. *An unpitied pain wins greater merit before God.* She turned and picked up a piece of chalk. It crumbled in her fingers, and she dropped the ashes of it in the cradle of the chalkboard, picked up another, and wrote, "A childhood memory." Then turned toward the class, looked at Carmelo still slumped, and said, "Write about something you remember from your childhood. Something that happened to you, or to someone else. But please do not write about love. I want to hear about an action."

Carmelo raised his head. He understood some of what his teacher said. Enough to know she did not want to know about love. And enough to know he was to write about being home. Something that happened. How was he ever going to write that? Making out with his Miguelina under the wraparound porch with Tia's chickens running in and out and interrupting them with their squawk, squawk, squawk, and their laughing between kisses and neck sucks. *Pero dice no escribe amor.*

***

Carmelo smoothed his hand across the paper on his desk. He liked what he wrote. It looked good on the paper. It's not love. It's Mami love. That's different.

He stood up, walked to the front of the room, and gently set the piece of paper with this different kind of love ideas written—written, wow, written—on it, smiled at the teacher, turned around, and walked back to his seat, glancing back and forth among his classmates with bent heads and stubby fingers making English words on line paper and thought how maybe he was becoming like them—a student!

"Carmelo!"

"*¿Qué?*" He turned around.

"Yes, Carmelo, you. May I speak to you here, back here at my desk?"

He walked back toward the teacher sitting like a nun behind her desk, looking at him like he was a mistake.

"This is a good try. But look at this word."

That's a red pencil going around a word on his paper, making a line of blood under his word.

"Say this word for me, please, Carmelo. I don't know what this word is."

¡Ella no sé una palabra English! He looked down at the line of blood and then at the word that it was bleeding on. "Dichoder."

"Say it again, Carmelo."

"Dichoder."

"It's not a word in English, I'm afraid."

"*Pero*, you teacher, you say it. I hear it. You say, 'give it you paper a dichoder.'"

"Oh! Yes. Each other. Yes, I do say that. But I do not put a *D* on 'each,' and I do not say 'oder' for 'other.' And this is how to write what you wrote."

She's turning his paper over. She's writing, what? "Each other." Now she's turning the paper back to the side it was on first and is moving her pencil around his word so that the blood is encircling it.

She wrote "each other" over the red puddle, and then she crossed out his "dichoder" that was now soaked in this teacher's blood.

He took his paper away from her and stood up. "*Gracias*," he said. But he did not feel like *gracias*.

Chapter 64

Recruitment of Faculty

Cardenias' policies adhere closely to the bylaws of the Board of Higher Education. Responsibility for selection of faculty members rests generally with the individual departments and, in particular, with the departmental personnel and budget committees, *and I'm so sorry, Professor Comen, that you were not included in this gathering, and I do thank you so much for the letter recommending me for reappointment in spite of this, even if it was only one sentence and gave me no meat and fodder for including it in my personnel file.* If budgetary considerations determined by the college-wide Personnel and Budget Committee permit approval of such positions, the department, this professor, can understand why Carmelo has such difficulties with . . . with just about everything, when he has a brother who . . .

Today after class, she'd do that right away. Today after class she'd do that, go back and check everything that would need to be edited out.

Chapter 65

"Oops!" Alma looked at the blank white screen in front of her. *Close your ears to the whisperings of hell and bravely oppose its onslaughts.*

She looked at Delores. She looked back at that stark white screen. "I've done it."

"What?" Delores looked up.

"I hit a wrong key. It's all gone."

"Uh oh! Don't touch anything. I'll go get Professor Alveraz. You know, the computer whiz. He teaches math . . . the math chair. Just don't do anything."

Professor Alveraz? Yes, Professor Alveraz. With the succulent voice that said, "So nice to see an attractive nun in this school."

"I'm a nun no more."

"Glad to hear it. Too attractive for a nun—at least the kind I grew up with." And then he had kissed her cheek and walked on. Now he would fix her computer?

Alma laid her forehead on the keyboard.

"Get your head up! You'll hit another key."

***

"I see our little nun in residence has a problem?" Professor Alveraz followed Delores into the room and Alma stood up.

"I . . . I am no longer—"

164

"I know, I know. Let me look at this. Do you know what key you hit?"

"No, no. It was on the left I think, but I don't know. It's my . . . it's the self-study report."

"Yes, I know. The dean was at the last meeting of the chairs. He said he is actually waiting for it. Deadline soon, I think he said. So, let's see."

Succulent voice, can he? Is he magic? *Suffering is a short pain and a long joy.*

"What's that Professor Hedman? I didn't hear you."

"Saint Henry Suso said that . . . and I really appreciate your help, Professor Alvaraz."

"Sure. I'll have your report back in no time."

And please, please don't read it when you get it back. "I'm in the process of editing it. I have a class."

"That's fine. Go to class."

Chapter 66

"Ah, here you are, Professor Hedman. Your report is back on your screen. It took a while. Some outsmarting technology I had to do, but it's back, so you have no worries. It's back. Except . . . well, I believe it's the self-study report that is back, but I did notice while I was checking to make sure it *was* the report which you had lost, which you said was the self-study report, yes, I did decide that what I was looking at was just that. Is something the matter, Professor Hedman? Are you all right? Can I get you some water? Here, I have a new bottle here. Why don't you take a drink?"

"Yes, thank you, Professor Alverez. You see, it's not edited." Alma gulped water from the professor's bottle. 'It still needs . . . it's just not edited yet."

"Oh. Well. That's a relief, I must say. Looks like it might take some heavy—"

"Yes, well . . . it will be easy to do. The italics will help. I still need to do the mission—"

"Um, I have to admit, you still seem . . . Here, Professor Hedman, have another drink."

Chapter 67

"Where is it, Carmelo?"

"*Pero* ..."

"*Don't 'pero' me!* You get it by tomorrow or you gonna blow up from bat's boils!"

"*Sí, sí,* Rudolfo." He got out of Rudolfo's truck. Why did he ever say yes to a drive to school?

"Remember ..."

Other words came from Rudolfo's truck as it drove off, but they mingled with "Carmelo! Carmelo, over here by the park!" And he looked over at the park. Nurys. Again? Already? Before class even? How did she know he was going to get out of that truck. Was she watching and he didn't see her?

"Come over here." Nurys kicked a beer can into the street and pointed to Capa Park behind her.

Carmelo watched her shadow wiggling next to her, snakelike, but did not move.

"I said *come here!*"

Did he have a choice? He stepped off the curb and crossed the street.

"I can see that other candy bar's still stickin' outta your pocket. So you must still be being rude to *mi tio* and ignoring him or sompin'. He said he'd buy it from you, but you won't go near to him. So, are you nuts? *Loco, loco, loco.* You'd better hide it if you gonna keep it. *Mi tio,* he's discreet—that you gotta learn. Come on, we got time. We go sit in the park. I like it. Not *too* garbagy."

Chapter 68

Lavender? For an observation? Too late now anyway. She should have thought about appropriateness twenty-four hours ago—twenty-four hours' notice. Please sign. Yes, she had gotten it, had signed.

"Thanks, and see you then. Room three twenty, right?"

"Right. Room three twenty." Carmelo's class.

Tomorrow, class, we will have a visitor. A colleague wants to see the class. Sit in on it.

What that, Teacher, 'sit in on'?

Sit here and listen.

You mean you be observed, right, Teacher?

Yes, Juan.

No worry. We all the time good, Teacher.

They *were* under control. So why was she shaking? They would be good. They were responsive. Most of the time. There would be no static electricity, and they have the nun business out of their minds by now.

Why you no a nun?

They ex-something you?

You divorce from God?

Maybe water. Maybe a walk down the hall. Maybe talking to someone. Where was Delores when she needed her? Tell her how she looked. Did she look neat? She was careful about that, about being put together. Style is important, she said. And she had suggested lavender once.

You're looking good these days, Alma. That's a good haircut for you. Makes your eyes—well, you are pretty, if you'd let yourself be.

So why was she shaking?

She opened the door, propped it with a chair, and walked down the hall. Her hands hugged each other at her waist. She stood in front of the cooler and prayed. "Lord, in thy mercy . . ." She unclenched her hands, picked up a cup, and felt someone close behind her.

"Why are you shaking so? What's the matter?"

This warm mellow voice . . . Professor Alverez?

"You seem upset?"

"I'm being observed next period."

"Oh. I never seem to get used to that either. You'll be fine." He touched her shoulder lightly and turned away, saying, "Don't hit any keys you don't mean to hit."

"Yes, yes, I know, and thank you again for—"

"Don't mention it. I like solving problems, but like I say, don't hit any keys you don't mean to hit."

"Yes, yes—I mean no, no, I won't."

The lavender was probably fine. A nice light lavender anyway, and the blouse was right—she knew that. Delores had said so, too, when she picked it off the rack at Macy's. And then that lipstick she'd made her buy. "Doesn't mean I'll wear it," she had said. "I know, but buy it anyway."

Chapter 69

Evaluation of Faculty

Faculty members are evaluated according to a negotiated agreement between the Board of Higher Education and the union. Every faculty member is observed once each semester by a member of his or her Personnel and Budget Committee or by faculty members so impaneled by that committee, *like Professor Comen must have been impaneled.* This observation is followed by a conference between the faculty member and the observer, providing the opportunity for a frank discussion of instructional techniques and other faculty responsibilities. *And her first question to Professor Hedman was whether she was going to publish at all, which Professor Hedman did not think had much to do with the class she had observed, which was primarily a review of the present continuous tense, after the papers describing an incident on the sidewalk in front of the school all seemed remarkably alike, both in content and in execution, and this professor inferred from the construction of the sentences that they had all been translated by the same person, and this issue was about to be discussed when brown liquid began pouring through the ceiling and Juan said "Photography lab baja above?" and Professor Comen made a face, screwing up her nose, so Professor Hedman said, in order to save the observation, "Class, what is happening right now ...," changing the projection of the discussion from accusation of plagiarism to a real time teaching moment by saying, "Think of the present tense, or better yet, think of the present continuous tense," but Professor Comen got up and left, because, she said, she had another appointment, but Professor Hedman knew it was because a student had questioned the appropriateness of a prior assignment, which he designated now as the possible cause for a "fucking street scene" just before the smelly brown liquid puddled extensively onto the floor.*

Chapter 70

"Thank you, class, for your cooperation the other day and for understanding the situation, more or less. And now that we have the various present tenses under our belts, let's move on to the past. Here is your assignment: 'My First Day in This Country'. *¿Comprendo?* I mean, *comprendez?* How you got here. Plane? Who met you? How did it feel? All of you have come from different places, as has been previously revealed by Juan, so all of your experiences of your first day here are probably very different. You've come for different reasons—some to get jobs, some to be with family—and you've left your countries for different reasons, some to ..."

Carmelo listened to this rattle of words. Some he knew, but there were lots of words in between that he did not know.

"... some to get away from poverty."

"Teacher, *qué es* 'under our belts'?"

"... as I say, some to get— Your question, Juan? Under our belts? Well, under our belts means ... means we're done with it. Just think, what is under your belt? Your stomach, right? So it must mean that whatever it is, we've ... we've swallowed it, finished it, digested it. Yes, that's it. We have digested the present tenses. In other words, learned it ... them. There is no need to giggle, class. Juan asked a reasonable question.

"Now, let's continue. You have all come here for different reasons. Carmelo, your hand is up. Do *you* have a question?"

"*Sí.*" He stood up. "*Todos mis problemas comenzaron ese dia. Todos mis problemas han sido desde ese dia,*" he said into the blank stares around him.

He heard himself and saw his arms wave. He tried to stop them from waving, put them in his pockets to stop the waving, and then pulled them out because he *had* to wave them to get his point across. He did not notice that when he did that, he brought something out of his pocket. It landed on the floor.

Nurys reached from her desk, swatted his arm, and whispered, "You idiot, pick that up! And why do you even still have it, stupid?"

Alma saw another confrontation in her classroom begin.

Be ye prudent as the serpent who, in danger, exposes his whole body . . .

"Speak in English, please, Carmelo and Nurys, if you must speak." She started to walk between the desks toward them. "And please pick up the candy bar that dropped out of your pocket, Carmelo, and remember I do not allow eating in class."

. . . to preserve his head.

The door opened. "Sorry to interrupt your class, Professor Hedman, but I never seem to reach you in your office, and it is necessary that the reaccreditation report be on my desk in two weeks, so thought I'd remind you. In addition, Professor Comen has informed me that she informed you of the necessity of your being enrolled in a PhD program immediately, and I do not see any indication of this on your observation report."

The door closed.

Alma turned around and walked back to the front of the class, dismissing the dean's interruption, but hearing again Professor Comen's post-observation conference statement damning her with faint praise. *I repeat, Professor Hedman, you may have passed the hurdle of your first observation minimally, but I have not heard that you have enrolled in that PhD program, which I advised, and the fact of doing the self-study is not an excuse to put it off.*

Once in the back of the room, she turned toward the class and said, "The past tense requires an 'ed' at the end of a verb on regular verbs. I still see your candy bar on the floor, Carmelo. As in 'open' and 'close,' for instance. The door just opened. Past, the door then closed."

Carmelo leaned down, picked up the candy bar, and saw himself as a very bad idea.

"Teacher, *qué es* 'for instance'?"

"What is . . . what did you ask, Juan?"

Carmelo stuffed it into his pocket and sent Oshun wishes to the garage man to buy this one too.

"For instance? For instance. *¿Qué es?*"

"Oh. For instance means . . . Did I say 'for instance'? I meant to introduce irregular verbs, verbs that are different from our 'ed' ones, like opened and closed, verbs that are individual, verbs that go their own way, verbs that are independent, verbs that don't care what the regular verbs think or do, verbs that break all the rules and so are called irregular, like do, did, done, and think, thought, and you learn them differently too. You have to sing them to yourself in the shower, like sing, sang, sung."

"Now we learn Chinese, *eh*, Teacher?"

"No, Juan, this is English."

Carmelo felt the candy bar in his pocket, along with a lot of sweat.

Chapter 71

"How's it going, Alma?"

"It's moving along, Delores. I just have to remember to do some . . . Obviously I still have to edit it."

"That shouldn't take long. Most of it was from notes you got from departments, so—"

"I know. I took some liberties with the language sometimes, so I have to make sure it's still accurate. But I've italicized the questionable spots, so shouldn't be too hard to delete. And I'm taking the GREs tomorrow. Did I tell you?"

"You'll do fine. Don't worry. We all went through that. I'm ABD, but I may not get around to the dissertation."

"And I have to finish this report, and the true apostolic life consists in giving oneself no rest or repose. Know who said that? Camillus de Lellis."

"What the devil is an apostolic life, and who the devil is Cam something . . . never mind. I don't really care. Nor should you, Alma."

Delores could be insensitive sometimes, Alma thought as she lay her head on the keyboard of the computer.

"Look out! You'll hit a key!"

Alma looked up and stared at the screen.

"Did you hit anything?"

"No, I don't think so. It's still here! Instead of getting tutored in math for GREs, I should be getting tutored in computer-ease for this self-study thing."

"Glad I'm not you."

"I'm sorry I am."

Chapter 72

Mami said be a priest. She didn't mean Catholic. She meant a *babalowas*, but he is not good for that. Miguelina, though, an angel, she could be orisha. She could make the saint, she is so good. "Carmelo, I forgive you," she says when he fucks up. *That* is being a saint. Even Mami never said, "I forgive you," so Miguelina is who he should be with.

Singing at her uncle's asiento that time, he did not stay for her singing. He left. And she went to him after, days after, and did not give him the eye, but looked at him instead with water from the gods brimming on her lids. She was so sad.

"No *escucha*," she said and buried her tears in his arms. "*Pero* I forgive you. *Yo te amo.*"

He'd better watch where he was walking, or he would walk in some dog's shit here in this city with its sidewalks covered with that and other crap—broken bottles, newspapers that people don't even read, but just throw down no matter what big news. Like that one: THE CITY OF APPALACHIA HAS NO MONEY.

Is he reading that headline right? "The City of Appalachia." Yes, he is. "*Appalachia es Pobre.*" How could a city not have money? Money was the reason he came to the city of money, which he knew now was not the city of the money. He knew before this headline that it was not the City of the Money. But that was why he had come, so he could get money, so he could earn it, so he could send it to Mami, so he could marry Miguelina, so they could live as King Carmelo and Queen Miguelina *en una cemento en San Juan,* and not in a wood house with a tin roof digging onions in a little town with nothing but mountains to look at.

"*O even uno cemento en San Juan,*" he said aloud to the headline, but not in a little town with nothing there to do but sell gasoline.

"Fuck!" He picked up the newspaper, rolled it up, and hit the subway wall all the way down the steps to the platform. *Wham! Wham! Wham!*

Appalachia has no money. Then tomorrow it will be Cardenias Community College has no money, and *mañana, mañana* Mario has no money, and *mañana, mañana, mañana, Carmelo Rodriguez 'll jamas jamas* have any money.

"Shit!" If the whole world is out of money, it wouldn't matter if he learned English or not.

He whacked at the subway wall. Money! He needed a new shirt. Shoes. These still had lizard dung in the creases. And he wanted a Subaru, or even just the engine.

Maybe he *should* join Nurys and her uncle.

No, he would get money from a real job. Maybe he knew enough English for the garage. No, the man said he didn't. Nurys was right.

And do you know what, Carmelo? Todos los classe escribe en English now, and speak too better and better every time, and you es tonto estúpido, pero you no even try. Mira, you no even say "yes" in English.

Why did Nurys care if he spoke and wrote in English? Only that man on Pike Street cared. But he would ask to see his diploma. He would want to know if he'd graduated. That would be how the man would know if he knew English. Not by listening to him talk.

"Hey, mister, I done graduated," he'd say. So he would know, but he would say, "Give to me. Show to me the diploma."

He swatted and whacked again at the subway wall.

But that was wrong anyway. That was nonstandard. *That's nonstandard English, students. I'm going to teach you standard English so that employers will hire you.*

Fuck the teachers anyhow. What do they know? They have jobs.

A piece broke off from the rolled up and torn newspaper and fell, floated to the floor.

Have graduated. That's it. Not done graduated. Hey, holy shit! That was that present perfect thing that the teacher was sticking into his head like mud.

He threw the newspaper over his head. It unfurled, separated, and fell to the floor.

I have graduated. Hey, mister, I have graduated. Or is it "has"?

He leaned down and picked up pieces of newspaper that had scattered into tents.

It es "has."

He put the pieces together to make a newspaper again.

That teacher was always saying something about third person singular. What was that? *He* was a third person, because *he* was over there, always in the corner of the room, away from *I* and away from *you*. That was have? Has? *Jesus, which is it?*

He held a piece of the newspaper in reading position and talked aloud to it.

"I has graduated—that not third person. I have. Yeah, it's 'I have.' That what people say, *pero* I hear they say 'he have it.' No, they say 'done,' but done no *es* correct, so it not that."

It was present perfect time. That he knew, because it was not just past, because it was still happening. He would always have his diploma. When he got it. *If* he ever did get it.

So it perfect present. Y no third person. First person, that it. I have graduated! Wow!

He should celebrate. Maybe a party. No, there is no place for that. Buy flowers. Yes, buy flowers. Where is one of the those flower guys? Buy some flowers for . . . me? No. For Maria? No, she like Rudolfo. For Nurys? No, she would decide he loved her. For Miguelina.

I have graduated. I have graduated. Holy shit! Miguelina, I have graduated y . . . and I send to you flowers! She will put them to her face. She will put them to her nose. She will stroke them and say, "From my Carmelo." Yes!

But Miguelina wasn't here. Only Nurys. Give Nurys flowers? No. She is nothing but trouble. But he did need to buy some flowers . . . for somebody. Teacher. Teacher Alma. Professora. Then she would say yes to his writing and give him an *A*. And he would graduate, and then the motor guy would say yes to his diploma and give him a job. And then . . . okay. But he would think about Miguelina with the flowers in his arms as he gave them to Teacher Alma.

Chapter 73

"I'm off to class, Delores."

Alma opened her office door and saw, running toward her, Carmelo carrying an armful of what looked like small red flags. She saw, too, right behind him, Professor Alverez—both going the wrong way. Both the classroom and Alverez's office were in the other direction. They both seemed to be heading for her. There were no other offices or classrooms near her office, only a staff rest room, so she had to be their aim.

She watched them come. Almost neck to neck. No, now Carmelo is winning. Uh oh, Alverez has passed him. No, neck to neck again.

She stood. Waited. Carmelo was probably going to bribe her with flags, and Alverez was ... what?

"Come, Professor Hedman, for coffee, or do you have class now?"

"Thank you, Professor Alverez, but I—"

"For you, *Professora*." Carmelo pushed ahead and thrust an armful of red into Alma's arms. "*Para Miguelina, pera—*"

"Oh my! Roses," said Professor Alverez as the roses collided with the two professors and Carmelo in an aroma-filled threesome, bathing them in blooms.

"*Para* Puerto Rican Culture Day. No, no, wait. In class, I give you in class," Carmelo said, looking at Professor Alverez. He wrapped his hands around the rose bundle, turned, and said, "See you in class, Teacher." He turned and trotted down the hall, hugging his gift.

"Well," said Alverez.

"Well," said Alma.

"I guess another time if you have class now."

"Yes, another time if I have class now."

"Do you?"

"What?"

"Have class now or not?"

"I do." *Let the world indulge its madness, for it cannot endure and passes like a shadow.* "Thank you."

***

Carmelo stood by the door, listening to his professor take the roll and holding close the bunch of red roses that were really for Miguelina, but maybe he should have let his teacher keep them back by her office. Except there was that other teacher, and this teacher might think the roses were from that other teacher, and if he had left the roses there with her like that, she would never remember him saying like he did, "Para Puerto Rican Culture Day," and she would think they were from that other teacher.

When she calls his name, he will go in. That will be the right kind of timing.

"Juan?"

"*Aquí* ... here."

"Mercedes."

"Here, Teacher."

"Carmelo?"

He opened the door and said, "Ah, Professor, *aquí*, presento ... here." He walked purposely and gallantly to the front of the class, handed the flowers to Professor Hedman, and said again, "Para Puerto Rican Culture Day."

Alma took the flowers, confused at receiving them twice, heard clapping from the class, and held them close until she felt prickles her arm. Why had she thought they were flags? Right up to the last moment of Professor Alverez saying "Well!" she thought they were flags.

"Thank you, Carmelo," she said, and wondered if she should see them as some sort of bribe and not accept them, but how could she, now having taken them, say "no thank you" and give them back, even though he had, sort of, done that with her, but not now, especially since Carmelo was walking to his seat, getting high fives and cheers as he went.

She set them on the desk, turned to the blackboard, and wrote her planned sentence for instruction: "Life is a long pain and a short joy." Or did the saint say, "Suffering is a short pain and a long joy? Or is it a short joy and a long pain?"

"Teacher, you mumble again."

"Sorry." It's quite simple. No subjunctive, just a subject and predicate. With the article. They know about them, even if they leave them off.

She erased the "and" clause and closed her ears to the grumble in the room.

"Teacher, qué es? What means . . . qué es 'pain'?"

Ah, a teachable moment, the prickles on the roses sticking her arm. Yes. What a great example. She picked up a rose, pointed to a thorn, pushed the thorn into her arm, and said, "Ouch."

"Teacher, you no like the rose?"

"No, no, Nurys. I love the roses. I'm demonstrating . . . giving an example of . . . of pain. The meaning of the word."

The door opened. The dean stepped through it. "Professor Hedman, may I see that first draft by Friday?" He stepped out. The door closed.

Alma stared at the door, turned toward the class, and said, "This is the title of your paper: Life is a long pain."

Chapter 74

I am Saint Clare of Assisi, and I am coming to you, Alma, in this dream to tell you to close your ears to the whisperings of hell and bravely oppose its onslaughts. And yes, that is a tree on your desk, and I am at your desk, and so is a man with a moustache, hunched over, working under the tree. Thick, succulent leaves are on the tree that is really a plant. A short tree, a plant, a succulent tree, a succulent plant, the thick, succulent leaves are at his forehead, a shade, shield, working at your desk under a succulent plant for now. Does he know he will have to give it up? Does he know the arrangement? That his thick-leaved succulent plant is temporary? It is HER desk, and upon her return, he will have to leave. He will have to take his plant. It looks so permanent, it looks so potted in the desk. It looks potted in dirt in the desk; it looks sunk in permanent earth in his most temporary desk, and it is HER desk. He cannot take the desk with him when he leaves. He cannot, he cannot, he cannot, and he will have to leave.

"Are you going on the march, Alma?"

Alma raised her head off her desk.

"You asleep?" Professor Alverez was a blur in front of her.

"I guess I was. And dreaming. Dreaming."

"Time to wake up. I said, are you going on the march?"

"What march?"

"On City Hall."

"March? On City Hall? Why?"

"There's talk of closing the college."

"I thought the funding had been restored." *No, it couldn't have been him. He doesn't have a moustache.*

"It's in question again."

"Why is moustache such a hard word for them? I used it the other day and couldn't explain it, and headache too."

"I don't know. They don't come up much in political science ... those words, I mean."

"I would think headache would. I guess it's the *che* sound. What is that in Spanish?"

"It doesn't exist, that combination of letters. Wait, yes it does. It means power, 'ache' is power. It's the power the orishas have .. and power, just 'power'."

"Orishas?"

"Deities. Don't worry about it. It's too complicated. How are you coming with your relationship with the computer?" He leaned over her shoulder and looked at the screen.

Alma looked up at him. He did have a moustache.

"Come on, before you hit a wrong key again and send the whole thing into space. Let's go for coffee before we don't have any money to buy it."

What, she wondered, did his mouth look like under the moustache? She couldn't tell; his top lip was completely smothered in hair.

Chapter 75

STUDENT CLUBS

Student clubs are considered a real and necessary part of college life. Clubs sponsor and promote such observances as Martin Luther King Jr. Day, Puerto Rican Culture Week, *which on Monday of that week Carmelo bought a dozen red roses with his rent money and gave them to his teacher, who used the prick of the needles to illustrate pain to the class. And if funding for the school is in question, then student clubs are also in question, and why wasn't she informed about this so as to deal with it in the report, and what was it she overheard in the hall about Carmelo being urged to do what?*

Need to get: details and programs of student clubs.

Chapter 76

Carmelo is on a bus. Why he isn't sure, except Nurys, Awilda, and Jose said if he didn't go to see the governor the college would close, so he got on the bus with them. Even the president said he had to go, because he wanted him to deliver something to the governor. He chose him, he said, "Because you are typical and you are tall." Typical sounded like a word in Spanish, and tall he knew, and he knew Mami would say, "Do it. The president said to do it. You obey the president."

So, okay, he is obeying. And sleeping. And dreaming. Of Miguelina. And she is sitting on the beach dreaming of him. Yes, she is sitting on the beach dreaming of him. *Carmelo, I do a love ebbó for you to come home, she is saying. I will put in this water the ebbó.*

She probably has already carved out a pumpkin, put in the five rooster toenails and the egg and the pepper and the other stuff Oshun would want, and she probably put in a sock she got from Mami, who would tell her how to do the pumpkin and how to offer it to Oshun and how long she should wait before throwing it in the river.

Carmelo, now you will come home in five days. And she will take a love bath for five days with these roses and honey and clove all boiled together, and she will smell like a piece of cloud from heaven, and then she will burn a yellow candle for Oshun. *Digame, mi Miguelina, do I say it right?* And all the time she is singing like a Madonna.

And El Carib said she was too young, and by now no way is she too young, no for El Carib and not for him either, but she never was too young for him, even when they were in seventh grade and they kissed in the rain forest that day.

But it all just means he needs money so she can come and play grown-up kissing games in his own house in the city of the money. *And then . . . and then when we are rich, we can go back, and our babies will play Dona Ana, looking at the mountains and that big wide sky.*

"Carmelo."

Somebody calling him out of his dream . . .

"Carmelo, wake up. We need for someone to speak to the governor. In Spanish. He speaks Spanish, and he *is* Spanish, so you are good for that."

"*¿Quién?*"

"Me. Juan. Come on."

"*Tambien*, you Spanish too."

"Yeah, but you elected to do this, and I don't speak Spanish that good."

"Come on, Carmelo. Do it for you *amigos.* Out on a balcony like. *Con una* microphone—big time, Carmelo."

Speech? Mami say obey, pero this not a president of the college, just president of students, pero a president.

***

Carmelo felt eloquent.

"*Alumnos, estan por cerrar nuestro colegio. Pero no lo lograran. Tenemos demasiado poder para ellow hacer eso. Pero hay dos puntos mas qué son y no son ralacionados. Es sobre la proposicion del aumento de la ensenanza—*"

"Hey, dude! You know everybody don't speak Spanish here."

"Oh yeah? This school for Puerto Ricans."

"Black is here too, so talk in English, man."

Could he say it in English? Did he know enough? Is that Juan running up here?

"What Carmelo here say, and then he say what he say before, *pero* I say it *ahora* one time. He talk about they put our tuition up. *Y* he no finish, he want to say to you governor, no close school!"

He looked over at Juan and let love for his fellow PR man swallow him. He looked out over the small crowd and felt good. There was Teacher Alma in the back. He would ask her how she liked his speech.

Chapter 77

SUDDEN BUDGET CRISIS

There continues to be a budget crisis, as there was the first year of the opening of the college. As back then, there is talk on the part of the city about closing this campus. This professor has received factual reports from departments that include such information, and will dutifully report in the appropriate place and manner. At present, students, faculty, staff, and administration, as well as community leaders and ordinary citizens, are participating in rallies at City Hall and in the State Capitol, *and, on the way to the Capitol, Carmelo slept and dreamed about Miguelina, and, as reported by a fellow student, was woken up and asked to speak at the rally in front of the governor's palace.*

Two thousand petitions have been presented to the mayor and to the governor, *and Carmelo was the one chosen to present them to the governor, and when he did, he accidentally stepped on the governor's foot. Carmelo will never forget that. He will die thinking of it. He tried to write about it in the "Most Embarrassing Incident assignment," but got no further than "I step on foot."*

The budget cuts are slashing, bit by bit, essential services like a doctor on campus, academic and career programs, the cafeteria, and around-the-clock custodial services. Career departments are being absorbed or eliminated, *and when Carmelo became aware of this, he knew that a motor repair division would never happen.* This resulted in an increase in the number of liberal arts students, *of which Carmelo is one, because he can't decide between hotel management and radiologic methodologies. The counselor told him he should be deciding, but if he couldn't repair motors, he didn't care what he did.*

Chapter 78

"*Ola*, Teacher?"

"Yes, Carmelo."

"You like my speech?"

"You spoke it in Spanish. I don't speak Spanish."

"No. Yes. I know that. *Pero* the English, it was good?"

"No, Carmelo. You don't understand. That's not how it works. You have to speak in English for me to say that your English was good."

"No, no, teacher. You no understand. My speech, it was good in English? It was a good speech in English?"

"Yes, your speech was a good speech in English if it had been in English. And now that that is over, how about getting the rest of your back homework done."

"*Qué*, Teacher? Back homework? *¿Qué es?*"

"Your past homework. What you have not done. What you owe me. You are behind."

"No, I am here. In your front."

"Carmelo, you know what I'm talking about. Stop playing the 'I don't understand your English' bit. Here is what you must do. I will give you the assignments again. One: grammar pages ten to twenty in your text. And the childhood memory paragraph."

"I do."

"Yes, but it was too short. You need to write more sentences. I know! Why don't you write about motors!"

"Motors, Teacher?"

"Yes, motors. I don't know about them."

"*Escribo* motors?"

"Yes!"

Carmelo nodded and left the room. How was he ever going to do that, write in English about motors when he had troubles bigger than ten coconuts and being the dead man walking that he was? From giving off vibes that he has money in his pocket—and not even his—and was Rudolfo even going to accept one-half kilo for the money he had given him, which was for a whole, which he didn't even have anyway.

Chapter 79

Professor Klinghoffen blew his nose.

Alma closed her eyes. *A PhD, Professor Hedman. You'll have to be in the process of getting it . . . but you won't make it here . . . don't know our students . . . a PhD . . . never will . . .*

She opened her eyes. Professor Klinghoffen was nodding his head toward the blackboard. She closed her eyes. *If you want tenure, Professor, you will have to at least be in a—*

Professor Klinghoffen blew his nose again and said, "A few words about cyclic rule ordering before we move on to identifying the null concept."

She opened her eyes and held her eyelids up with a finger, one finger on each, and heard Professor Klinghoffen say, "The noun phrase that is triggering . . ."

She let her fingers drop and her lids closed again. Images formed. She watched them lodge and dislodge, form vignettes, un-form, lengthen into stories, abort, become memories, fill out, extend themselves, become people—Mama, Delores, Father William—sitting across from her, his vestment hugging his belly.

You seem to be interested in words, Alma, why don't you consider linguistics? It's a fairly new field of interest and . . .

She opened her eyes. Professor Klinghoffen was dropping his handkerchief into his briefcase and saying, "Given these sentences, plus passive, show first of all that cyclic rule application correctly accounts for it. For instance, 'John believed himself to have been loved by Mary.' Or 'Mary was believed by John to have loved her.' Now, the null concept . . ."

Carmelo believed himself to have been loved by . . . by . . .

"A sentence is never ambiguous in context."

Alma wrote that sentence down in her notebook, but its meaning fell into the inkwell and drowned.

Chapter 80

OPTIMISTIC STUDENTS

Before concluding with the mission of the college, it is necessary to emphasize that, in spite of a dedicated faculty and staff, and despite also a lack of adequate funding because of misconceptions concerning available funds—which has happened—and because of inconsistencies in communication between the administration of the college and the funding office of the city, the students are experiencing a hopeful and illuminating educational experience, *including Carmelo, who is faithful in attending the anger control sessions, this professor has been told, although not by him, and is willing to master irregular verbs.*

Chapter 81

A motor decil es mismo . . . Same . . . no, the same.

A motor decil . . . No, decil motor es . . . no, it . . . the same qué . . . that . . .

Motor . . . motor . . . gasoline.

Pero . . . pero no tiene un carburador . . . But no have . . . has . . . have un . . . a . . .

"Shit!"

Carmelo broke the pencil.

Just because he knew about motors did not mean he could write about motors. And why anyway? So that the teacher could know about motors? What did she care?

Explain it to me, Carmelo. I don't know about motors.

"Okay, bro. Whaddya doin' sittin' at Maria table and writin' all over it?"

"No escribo *on* the table, Mario. Escribo *on* papal, hermano *estúpido.*"

"Don't you call me stupid *cuando* you got *pasteles y* a bed a *sleepo* on."

"Mario, *professora es* comin' down on me. I got a write."

El . . . the piston, it . . .

"*Bueno, bueno, bueno.* I get a beer and you do the scribble."

El . . . the piston, it . . . hay una explosion . . . causa compression y la sparka pluga . . . the piston, it fit perfectamente . . .perfecto . . . en la chamber, and it move . . .

It move . . . that the right word? Move? Move? Yeah, that the look, but it no the pronouncement. Move . . . move . . . yeah! Move! Inglish have *E* silencio, the quiet *E*. Move, move, move. Yeah!

The piston, sé mueve 'pa riba y 'pa bajò . . . it move high and down . . . high? No, up . . . up. Up and down . . . up and down.

"Holy shit! I do it. I make it right!"

The piston move with . . . No.

At . . . No.

To the high . . . No.

Top.

Sí hay un temblequeo . . . If they is . . .

"Okay, so what you writin' 'bout?"

Tembloroso . . .

"Huh? Tembloroso? What the fuck? What you teacher wanna know 'bout tremblin'?"

"*¿Cómo sé dice 'temblar' en English, Mario?*"

"*Quando* when I done my beer, *pregunta*. What you writin' 'bout, anyway? *Tremblar?* Tremble . . . no, shiver. *Cómo este.*" Mario shook his beer can. "Yeah, I know, orgasm *problemente.*"

"Orgasm? Don't that mean the other thing?"

"You writin' 'bout love?"

"No. Motors."

"With you, that love."

"*Motors!*"

"Okay, motors. Then 'orgasm' ain't right. What you writin' about motors for?"

"The teacher, she want a know about motors. She no understand motors."

"Do you homework. I drink my beer."

"Yeah, *pero* she no understand."

Es necessario qué el combustible sea puro.

Is necessary qué . . . that . . . for. . .
fuel decil . . . decil fuel . . . es . . . is . . .
pur e . . . pur e . . . no, the quiet e—pure.
Cómo Miguelina.
"*Cómo Miguelina?*"

"What the fuck? You readin' ese? Thought you was over there drinking you beer. What you doin' sticking you head over me shoulder?" He pushed his elbow into Mario's stomach.

"Ha! You *is* writing 'bout love."

"This a first writing, and you . . . *hijo de la gran puta—maricón . . . y tu madre.*"

"Hey, *su madre es* my *madre.*"

"I no gonna fight *con* you *ahora.* I no *quero.*"

Carmelo spat small swear words at Mario and rolled his paper into a ball. "*Cómo* Miguelina" was right, and he knew what he was saying, and he knew why he was saying it. And of course he wasn't going to include that in his composition for the teacher, but if he wanted to write it, then, at that moment, it was right and none of fucking Mario's fucking business.

He spat some more swear words and opened the ball of paper, smoothed it on the desk, put his index finger and thumb low on the pencil stub, as near to the point as he could get them, and put his face as close to the paper as he could get it and still see the words. The spark plugs were next. And the explosion. How was he going to explain that? Did the teacher even know what spark plugs were? Did he need to define them? Jesus!

Miguelina knew. He talk about motors with her all the time. She even asked him a question once. Once when they were waiting for a bus and a huge motherfucker of a truck stopped and sat in the bus stop—a refrigerator truck that had on the side, "*Cremo y leche de la Evaristo y Peche.*" She had wanted to know why that monster—she called it a monster, and he guessed it was, but it was a beautiful monster, almost like the first one of those giants he saw back in Arecibo, a beautiful monster—she wanted to know why little tiny explosions came out of the chimney, she called it, in the back, and he explained it, and she listened.

That monster in Arecibo, he was so little and it was so big, he remembered. He was the height of the front wheel, and the driver looked out at him, at him staring up, and said, "You want a ride, kid?" That was the beginning. That was the beginning of falling in love—yeah, falling in love. That's what he did. He fell in love on the way up the side of that monster, that beautiful monster, through the door that the man opened and leaned out of, reached down from and grabbed him on the way up, helped him climb in, and lifted him over the steering wheel and into the seat. Then the man started the engine, and the explosion made him jump and shiver and shake. He thought a war had come and the man was a general and he was a soldier—and he was ready for it—and he pointed his finger out the window and said "bang bang," and the man laughed and said, "That's it, kid. Get 'em!"

He put his forehead on his paper. Sometime, when he knew perfect English, he would write that for the teacher, for that other childhood memory assignment that she did not like because it had a "dichoder" in it. And when she said, "I know you remember more than that you love your mother and that she loves you, which is wonderful, but what is something that happened?", he never knew what she meant, but now he knew what she meant. He never wanted to leave that truck seat, but the man said he had to go. He did not want to kidnap him, he had said.

He raised his head. He wished the man *had* kidnapped him. Then maybe he would be fixing diesel motors right this minute, instead of sitting at Maria's kitchen table smelling Mario's beer and trying to write in another language about his love so that some teacher could write all over it with blood and change it and make it the way she wanted it, when it wasn't even her that it happened to. But she did seem to want to know about motors.

La sparka pluga . . .

Chapter 82

Conclusion

To wrap up this report, a concise statement of the mission of Cardenias Community College is appropriate. The college's purpose was, and is, to provide career and liberal arts educational opportunities, *not including classes in repairing diesel motors as has been requested,* such as secretarial studies, history, and the social sciences, along with English, both literature and grammar, speaking and writing, for residents of East Park, Outerbridge, Canal Island, and other parts of the city that have economic and cultural barriers to higher education. The college was deliberately located, as stated in the opening paragraphs of this report, at its inception, *three blocks from Nurys's house and one subway ride from Carmelo's, which meant the meetings of these two were generally in Capa Park across the street from Carmelo's subway stop. Often the two would spend time before their class in English grammar and writing, passing little notes, teasing and flirting with each other in youthful gaiety,* to meet the needs of the residents of this economically depressed area and help them to achieve socio-economic mobility. This has continued to be an active goal of the college, while at the same time recruiting and attracting students from Central and

South America, *including Norman who fought with rebels, and Jesus who fought with the conservatives,* some Haitian and one Russian, two Poles, including whites. *Carmelo did not have much to do with the Haitians or Russian. He counted only two Anglos one semester in his English class. One sat in the back corner of this class and didn't say much, except that Nam was a fuckin' mistake. Carmelo was glad that he had been too young for Vietnam, and hoped he would be too old for whatever would come next.*

Chapter 83

"*Ola,* Teacher. I no have—"

"I don't have . . ." Alma sat down at her desk.

"No, no. *Tambien* I *do* has . . . have it, the homework. *Es* 'bout motors."

"Motors? You did it, Carmelo?"

Carmelo unfolded three pieces of white notebook paper. He handed them to the teacher and said, "*Sí*. You say . . . you no *sé* motors explain at . . . to me."

"Oh, yes. Of course. Good. Thank you. I shall read it tonight."

"*Sí, sí*. Yes. *Es* about motors. Like you say."

"Yes, good."

"*Pero* . . ."

"Yes?"

"*Es* explain about motors."

"That's fine."

"Teacher, you like motors?"

"I don't know about motors, so I am interested."

"Okay. Because *es* about motors *y* . . . and . . . about a man and a truck. He, the man, give me . . . put me up and up into his truck. *Es* history, too, Teacher, like you say before, a memory childhood."

"Is this about you?"

"I am . . . was a *bambino, sí, pero es* about . . ."

He had worried and worried about that, but the writing had happened that way—not just how a motor works—and he had liked the way it happened. It surprised him. He had not meant to do it that way, but then on the paper he was telling the story of the man in the diesel truck, and he didn't know he could do that, but he did. He had.

"And the title is 'Cremo *y* Leche de la Evaristo *y* Peche'?"

"*Sí. Es nombre en el* truck."

"I shall read it tonight, and we will talk about it tomorrow."

"Um . . . *tambien ahora?*"

"Do you want me to read it now, is that it?"

"*Sí.*" He watched his fingers dance in tiny rhythms on her desk.

Alma also watched his fingers dancing on her desk. She pushed herself back in her chair. She lifted his paper off the desk. She held it in front of her.

Carmelo watched her closely, intently. Mami could not see too well like that, like his teacher, holding his paper close like that to her eyes, he thought, and had to hold papers close to her face too. But the teacher could see okay, he knew.

But now she has picked up a pen! To write? To correct? Like before with his word *dichoder*? "No, *Professora, por favor,* no correct, read—*solimente.* No correct *ahora* . . . now . . . *favor?*"

Alma looked up. Carmelo's eyes were like darts. He looked wild. "All right. I will read it now." His anger level was low, she thought, and *it would be prudent.*

"I come back," Carmelo said to the back of his paper and got up. Calm. He knew he was calm. He walked to the window. He could see in his head what she was reading:

I had six years. I took love for big truck causa el senor man drive invite me to truck. Up, up, up I go. In el window. El senor man start motor. Boom, boom, bang. I like in a war, y feel excite . . .

"This is very nice, Carmelo. It is a very big improvement."

He walked back and sat down by the desk. "You finish?"

"No, not yet."

"Okay." He did not get up, but stayed, his eyes on his paper. He tried not to drum his fingers. That might make her stop reading.

Alma read aloud. "I take my finger to the window and I bang boom and the *hombre dice*, 'Go get 'em' in Inglés, and I know, *comprendo*, the English. Then the man say in mine language about the motors. The motor diesel gasoline and the motor gasoline are *mismo pero differencio*.

"Carmelo, this is excellent. 'So the piston fits into the . . . what? I can't read that word."

"It fit like this. *Perfecto*." He pushed his thumb into his closed other hand. "And if it no fit *perfecto*, it make shake," and he stood and shook his body, then sat down again.

"Oh. I see. So the perfect fit prevents vibration. Now I know something I did not know before. Thank you, Carmelo."

"No, *gracias*, Teacher. You teach. I know to write now." He felt himself bounce in the chair, and heard himself repeat, "I know to write. I know English. I can get job. I can go back to PR." He leaned across the desk. He watched her read and read, and when she looked up, he knew that she had finished the last words, "spark plug."

"Carmelo, you have an *A*," she said.

He leaned further across the desk and kissed her on her cheek. "*¡Gracias, gracias!*" He moved his kiss to her mouth, and then he left the room with a bubble as big as a balloon in his chest.

Alma dropped her bottom lip. She put her hand on her stomach to calm it.

That was a kiss. On her mouth. Not a Father William one on her cheek. It was certainly, entirely his advancement. Wasn't it? She had done nothing to bring it about. Or had she? She couldn't remember, or even figure out. She had merely read his paper and commented, said it was an *A*. And suddenly, there was his mouth. She had done nothing out of the way. Or had she? She had not. She had not gone over the bounds at all. Maybe she had when she held his head that time, but he was close to unconscious and needed care.

And now, how was she to act toward him in class, out of class? Did he now consider her someone other than his teacher? Was it a . . . an invitation that she had sent? Naturally she would not accept an invitation, but was it one? Of course. He loved her. And that was the bottom line, from which all actions would now follow. *You who do truly and earnestly repent you of your sins and are in love and charity . . .*

She stood up. She leaned against the file cabinet and tried to stop the rising and rolling waves that were rippling in her chest. "No, let it happen, let it happen," she whispered, somehow knowing that this was falling in love, not with Christ, but with a real person.

She should settle the floating. She should go home. Somehow go home. *Do not let the false delights of a deceptive world deceive you.*

"Yes, Clare of Assisi, you are right, but . . . but this was not false, not deceptive."

She'd better wait to leave. It all might show, and the world should not know that she had just fallen in love.

***

"I saw that, you *tonto*, stupid. I saw that kiss."

"Nurys!" Carmelo leaned against the hall wall and waited for Nurys to pass. "It *nada, nada, nada. Elle—*"

"No matter. You kiss the teacher, you kiss me."

She pulled him into a storage closet and closed the door. She put her hand on his chest. He felt a surge and put his hand on *her* chest. He squeezed what was under his hand, then moved his hand to her neck and down the neck of her blouse, and then under it and got some of that delicious flesh in his palm. And squeezed, squeezed, and then rounded the deliciousness in his palm until she moaned, and then he found her mouth.

Stop. Stop. He should stop! But he did not listen to himself.

Then a hand brushed his groin and made him yell, "Lemme outta dis closet! *Dega me salir el de este armario.*"

"I no keep you here," Nurys said, and moved her hand to his belly and planted it there, then pushed him to the floor.

***

Alma pushed herself away from the file cabinet and walked toward the door and out into the hall. She ignored the ruckus of noise in the storage closet from which she had found a small broom with which to sweep rose petals from her desk.

***

In the closet that Alma was passing, fingers were dancing like frogs up and down Carmelo's leg as he lay on the floor. Again, he yelled, "Lemme *vente!* Lemme outta this closet!"

"Okay, you turkey! I said, I no keep you here." Nurys got off of Carmelo, stood up, and put her hands on her hips. She looked down at him, spun around, opened the door, and went through it. It banged shut.

"*¡Dios mío!*" Carmelo said into the dark.

The door opened. "Get up! We finish this." She pulled at him until he stood. She pulled him from the closet into the hall. She pushed him into the nearest office and against the desk.

"Hey, this my teacher's room. We can't—"

She leaned against him, put her hands on his face, leaned forward, and kissed him, her tongue slobbering in and out of his mouth.

***

Alma stopped at the water fountain. Water would help wash away the tide that was still tormenting her with pleasure. She let water slide down her chin and run into her neck. She stood still, remembering the rose petals on her desk. She should have saved them, brushed them into her bag so she would have them forever.

Her bag! Wait! Her bag. It was still on her desk. And she had not locked the office door.

***

Alma walked into the room. "Oh dear! Oh dear! Children, *children*, what are you doing?"

Carmelo and Nurys broke apart.

Saint Fabiola had to do public penance because she took a consort . . .

"Sorry. Sorry, Teacher. Didn't see . . . come on, Carmelo, let's get outta here." Nurys pulled Carmelo toward the door. They both went through it.

Alma stood still. Her fingers wobbled on her desk and her feet glued themselves to the floor.

***

Public penance. public penance. Alma gathered her papers and undid her feet from the floor. She walked through the door and down the hall. She was somehow going to have to ... have to do something about her ... her defiled desk. She reached the water fountain, leaned over it again, and drank. *Draw near with faith, drink this in remembrance of me* ...

She let the water course along her forehead. Carmelo's kiss stung her lips again. She took another drink and allowed the water to fill her mouth. First a mission. Yes, first a mission. Follow them. Follow them. Follow the two desk defilers.

Chapter 84

Alma's shoes clicked in the corridor as she walked hurriedly to catch up to the couple ahead of her, yet not catch up, because, of course, to be seen by them—following them—would be catastrophic.

The temple of the spirit is raised through suffering . . . work or suffering, and suffering counts for more than work.

Up ahead, that *is* them. Turning the corner. It is . . . no, don't call. Be quiet and follow them. Catch up. Quickly, go . . . hurry!

Click. Click.

Let him see you, let him see you see him with her. Hurry. Before they . . . before. Okay, not the elevator, down the stairs, together, talking. He's saying . . . he's saying what? Too far away. And she's looking and laughing . . . and . . . make him see her see them, so he knows her pain. Catch them. Catch them!

Find sweet springs of piety amid the world's salty waves. . .

Click. Click.

Down the stairs too, around the bends after them, around the bends, closer now. Almost in a minute she will say, "See Carmelo? I see you and you see me, so you know I know of your infidelities. But look, you love me, and now you see that you love me, because I see you and you see me see you.

Fly through flames of earthly lusts.

"Hello, hello? Do you see me? Hello, Carmelo. Hello."

Without burning the wings of its holy desires . . .

211

May it please the mother of God . . .

"Hello?"

An unpitied pain wins greater merit before God.

"Hello, Carmelo. Did you know that suffering is a short pain and a long joy?"

The young man turned around.

"Oh, you are not. I thought you were . . . you are not. May you and your lady . . . I go now. Good bye. Carmelo. Goodbye. You are not Carmelo. Goodbye."

"What?"

"That is why I say goodbye to you. You are not Carmelo."

"What the . . . ?"

"Goodbye." She walked on, her heels clicking and Saint Fabiola warning public penance.

She walked slowly, her head down, watching each one of her steps. Step by step. Interesting floor—such an old old building. Used to be a factory, so still a factory, like the floor, and the walls—so terribly concrete.

"You okay?"

Was that Professor Alverez's voice coming from this concrete wall?

"You hoo? My pretty nun, I said, you okay?"

On a mission, yes, but what was the mission? Yes, to follow them. She looked up. Professor Alverez seemed to have horns. "Yes, thank you. I'm fine. I'm on a . . . mission—or I was."

"Yes, I have a class too, but saw that you seem to—"

"Yes, my class. I forgot. I have a class." She tried to get by him, but he seemed in a compressed and compromising position, and she had to stop and correct it. He was becoming entangled. Her mission, whatever it was, would have to wait.

Every creature in the world will raise our hearts to God if we look upon it with a good eye.

But his confusion did need to be clarified. Yet, her mission . . . Yes, she needed to catch up to those—that couple—and she did, but it was not the right one, and this *did* need attending.

"Professor . . . Excuse me. I mean—"

"Yes?" he turned, standing upright now, but still entwined, and with his horns protruding.

"Why are your hands shaking? Mira, eat something." He held out to Alma a small open bag of Fritos. They seemed to come from the innards of the chair he was entangled in.

"No, no, thank you."

"*Toma*. I don't want it." He put the bag into Alma's hand.

Take, eat, do this in remembrance of me . . .

"No, thank you. I'm not hungry."

He squeezed himself between the lowered iron bar and the seat portion of the chair, being especially careful to keep his long, curled horns from dislodging the bar—a goat? Squeezing in too small a space, determined anyway?

"There are too many chairs in the hall," he said. "Belong in my classroom here. I'm short of chairs."

"Oh."

She realized that what she saw was not what she saw. She had fused Professor Alverez and the chair into many forms and positions as he carried the chair over his head, with one upstretched arm holding a bag of Fritos, into Room 227 and swung it over, around, and down and placed it in the front row just visible to her as she peered into the room, extending the front row one chair size more toward the door. Now he was turning and coming out of the room, having rid himself of those horns. She managed to recreate the entanglement in her mind enough to satisfy herself that she had not been hallucinating.

"Are you sure you are all right? You are . . . well . . . standing. Thought you said you had a mission, a class. Let me—"

He put his hand on her forehead. The touch was cool and sweet. She leaned into his hand.

"A little warm, but doesn't seem feverish."

Draw near with faith, receive the hand, the words, the wafer. It is mete and right so to do.

She moved away from his hand and said, "Yes, yes, I'm fine. And you are right. I do have a class. Good bye."

"Feel better. Good bye."

Her mission. Her mission had failed. Saint Fabiola has failed.

Chapter 85

If a surge means love, then does he love *two* women? *¡Oh Dios mío! ¡Mami! Mami, what do I do?* She say, "Don't go by no surge, like you call it, *mi bambino*. Choose by asking, 'Is she clean? She can cook? Do she listen to you?'"

Okay, Mami, l'otra pregunta: do she fuck with drugs? *¡Miguelina no, pero ella aquí y Miguelina no aquí!*

But she forgives. But he'd better get back to her before she forgets how to forgive!

Chapter 86

Carmelo's kiss still would not go away. It lay on her lips, stinging, caressing, blistering. Only a real love kiss would hang on, lay like soft powder.

Time for class. This kiss has to go away. No, stay. A knock? Is that a knock on the door? Now? And opening?

"Teacher, I come. *Porque*—"

"Yes, Carmelo. It is you. You have come."

"*¿Sí, porque?*

"Yes, *porque.*" She put her hand on his arm, on his head.

He jumped back and said, "*Porque mi* bookbag. Teacher, you see *mi* bookbag? I leave it here yesterday. You see *mi* bookbag?"

His bookbag? His bookbag! There was no kiss. He wanted his bookbag. There is no—

"Teacher, you see my bookbag?"

"No, Carmelo. I didn't see. I don't see a bookbag."

"Okay. Maybe the libraria. I look. The motor diesel paper is good, right, Teacher?"

"Yes."

"A mark. Teacher? You give it the mark?"

"I did. I say it has an *A*, but I will look at it again, and maybe change. I don't know."

"We are friends, Teacher, remember? Remember?"

"I remember."

"So we are friends and the mark *es bueno?*"

"Yes, we are friends." *And I love you, Carmelo, and you do remember that you do love me.*

"I check it out in libraria." He walked toward the door. "It have . . . No, it has in it my books."

The soul cannot live without love. All depends on providing it with a worthy object.

Chapter 87

"Good afternoon, class. I don't want any surprises. Today we will . . . By the way, I may have to let you out early."

"*Qué es*, Teacher?"

"What is what, Awilda?"

"Surprises, you say, you no want it."

"That's right. I don't want any surprises. I don't want the unexpected. I don't want anyone to say, 'I didn't do my homework,' or 'I can't come to school tomorrow.' Or 'I have to leave early,' or 'I have an appointment in half an hour,' or 'I lost my papers,' or 'I did the wrong homework,' or 'I wrote a story instead of the assignment,' or 'yes, I wrote a long, long, long story instead of—'

Oh my! Carmelo is here.

"Yes, Awilda, your hand is up?"

"Teacher, *qué pasa*? You . . . you have vibrate."

"No, no. I'm fine."

"Surprise? ¿*Qué es?*"

"Nothing. Don't worry about it. It means 'the unexpected.' It means 'listen to me.' It means 'this isn't what I've been talking about, but it is what I'm thinking now, and it means I'm changing the subject from what I was talking about to something else.' I was talking about the unexpected, but now I'm talking about the expected, so if I have to leave early, here is the homework."

Alma turned and faced the blackboard and picked up the chalk. She held the chalk so that the tip of it pointed to the board, but she saw nothing come from the tip touching the board. So she put the chalk down, turned around, and looked at her class. She looked long and silently at the asientos in the back row, their white clothes gathering shadows as the sun inched bit by bit across the window. The class was silent. Why?

Then Juan said, "Teacher, *qué pasa?*" and she knew she had to speak. "How sweet it is to suffer," she said and left the room, hearing as she left, "Teacher, you talk low. You say something?"

She *must* purify her desk.

Chapter 88

FINAL CONCLUSION

It is clear that funding for this school is at best minimal, as the economy worsens *and dives to the bottom of the rain forest, as Carmelo so eloquently put it after he saw the latest headline.* It is now reminiscent of the initial financial crisis, when halls were being used as classrooms. It was found then that without area designations, students were not only interrupting classes in session, but confusing the desks and chairs meant for instruction with desks and chairs for lunch and lounging. *Carmelo and Nurys, in particular, confused these areas for intimate tête-à-têtes, which developed into more and more out-of-the-way intimacies, to the extent that this professor's desk became a platform for even greater boundary disruptions.* It is the mission of the college to ensure that all students develop their individual capacities and return to their own communities better able to contribute to them, *which does not seem to be what is in Carmelo's head at all. He does not want to go back to Barranquitas. He is torn between his love for two women—three actually, one of whom is his teacher, who found it necessary to twice cancel a class. First, to follow the retreating couple in order to prevent further deeper intimacies, and the second time to cleanse her office desk in whatever manner possible.*

Chapter 89

"Purify it."

As long as we have peace with the natures of this world, we are enemies of God.

"Purify what, Alma? What are you talking, mumbling, about?" Delores walked further into the office, over to her desk, pulled her chair out, and sat down.

"Purify it!"

This world and that to come are two enemies.

Delores leaned down and untied a sneaker. "Quit mumbling and tell me what this is about."

"Purify this ... this ... my desk."

"I don't do that sort of thing," she said, taking her sneaker off.

"Who does?"

"What's the matter anyway?" She untied the other sneaker.

"They were all over it."

"Who? What?"

"Carmelo and Nurys. Doing I don't know what, on my desk—all over my desk. That's the only way I can work. What did you tell me about those saints, those asientos? They can perform ... do stuff like that? Cleansings?"

"You mean when Í was talking about my son and my uncle?"

"Yes, a while ago." Alma picked up the phone. Dialed.

"Who are you calling?" Delores kicked off the other sneaker.

"Security."

"Is this Carmelo you mentioned the one who brought you roses?"

"Yes, yes." Alma hugged the phone under her chin and swept two dried rose petals from her desk onto the floor. "Nobody ever sent— Hello, Security? . . . nuns roses. Security? Why don't they answer?"

"Alma, you're out of your mind. And Security will think that too. Just what were they doing on your desk, anyway?"

"You know. Mouth stuff. More. *Why* don't they answer?" She slammed the phone down. "And he has a girlfriend in PR, and Nurys has no business . . . and I need my desk purified. You said something about *ebbós*, remember?"

"I said I don't do that. I'm going for coffee. You'd better come with me and calm down."

"No no. I can't."

"I can't leave you like this."

"It's okay. I'm calm. Go ahead. Don't worry."

"You sure?"

"Yes. Go. Go."

"Whoops, not in bare feet though." She leaned down and put her sneakers back on. "See you—and take it easy."

Alma stood rigid. Saint Teresa went barefoot. Not all of the saints did that. Just the discalced ones, the ones who needed to bare their feet.

She leaned against the file cabinet. *Blessed be those who follow the barefoot Teresa. Blessed be those who purify reports. Blessed be the peacemakers who leave in bare feet. Blessed be the poor in spirit who call upon the babalawos to administer the rites of the sacrament of the holy supper to purify the souls in Jesus Christ and purify reports and the desks on which the kisses of rapture descend to the valleys of deaths.*

Alma stepped away from the file cabinet. She looked at her rumpled desk. She gathered books and papers and put them on the windowsill.

Saint Agatha, that martyr, cut off her breasts and carried them around in a dish. Maybe if she'd had a Santera instead of being a saint, she would not have cut them off.

Research. Research. She'd have to find out about these cleansing people and *ebbó* stuff and Santeras.

Chapter 90

COUNSELING

The Counseling Department holds regular staff meetings, which all counselors are required to attend. A variety of issues and concerns with regard to the students are discussed, with some sessions devoted to analysis of specific counseling cases, *such as Carmelo and Nurys's involvement in I don't know what, and they haven't ended up in counseling yet that I know of, but that is where they surely should be.*

Faculty sponsored in-service training sessions are offered by the various academic departments, *and this professor is not sure what to make of the advances of Professor Alverez. And his references to me as the "sweet little nun" are also distracting from teaching and from writing this self-study report, which is sorely in need of a saint to make it come out right, and as for my desk and my . . .*

Chapter 91

Delores stood by Alma's desk. "Tell me—while you are editing, deleting, or whatever you are doing that's making you mumble all that weird saint stuff—do you think I could deduct the gringo tutor on my income tax?"

"Because he's a gringo or because he's a tutor?"

"You know what I mean."

"I guess if you can deduct your kid's education, you can. I don't know about that. By the way, I called the person you told me about, so don't be surprised if you see someone cleansing . . . fooling around with my desk."

"Good God! You're doing that?"

"I have to, Delores."

"It's not cheap, you know."

"I know, but I can't work here. Can't think. Have to do the Counseling Department. Left it out. Have to add it. Have to think it through. Not an easy one."

"Don't know what would be more complicated about that more than any other department. I'm off to class. Think about whether or not I can make that deduction. And can't believe you are getting a—" Delores shook her head and left the office.

Alma stared at the closed office door. Why did Delores think she would know about deductions? She didn't know about deductions any more than Carmelo knew about . . . knew about irregular verbs, any more than she knew about writing self-studies, any more than her mother knew about purification cloths, any more than she knew how to purify a defiled desk. But the babalowa person would.

Chapter 92

"Looks like it happened, huh, Alma?" Delores waved her hand at Alma's desk.

Alma looked at where Delores's hand was fluttering. "Why?" she said. "How can you tell? You mean because there is nothing on it? I took everything off beforehand."

"Look. Right there. Looks like a dove feather. See?"

Alma followed Delores's look, and yes, there was a small white feather teetering on the corner of her desk.

"Probably a Santera. How much did you pay? You going to let her read the coconut for you? Huh?"

"You sound sarcastic, Delores."

"No, no, no. Hey, each to his own. I left all that behind. Even being a Catholic, left that too. See . . ." Delores's voice trailed into silence as she sat down at her desk, leaned down, and took her shoes off.

Alma picked up the feather and gently laid it on the windowsill next to her pile of papers and books. "Just so I can work here, that's all I want. My work space needs to be organized and clean," she said, but Delores, she could tell, was not listening.

Chapter 93

"I know you have to feel all right about your desk. I understand that. It's like . . . well, all I know is, I just had a lousy class. Nobody, nobody had done the homework and— What's that next to your foot? Guess it's the *ebbó*."

Alma looked down. "So that's what's smelling. Smells like cinnamon."

"Guess she left it for Oshun, the Santera I mean. But you have to perform it."

"What do you mean?"

"Since you've already begun the process, you might as well finish it."

"You mean I shouldn't leave a sacred rite hanging?"

"Whatever. If I remember right, you have to write his name on a piece of brown paper and put it under the dish. Then in five days take it to the river with five cents."

"His name on a piece of paper? Whose name? What river? I just wanted my desk—"

"Any river. I don't know. I guess it doesn't matter."

"This is crazy. Anyway, there is no *his* name to write."

"I'm just the messenger. But my feeling is, you got your desk purified, or cleansed, right? Why not follow the whole thing through? Why do it half way? There's something going on with you besides a . . . an unclean desk. Like you just said, you can't leave a sacred rite hanging."

"Yes, one has to finish things."

"I have to go. My kid's waiting for me. I think he needs only a couple of more tutoring sessions, 'cause he's starting to speak Spanish again. See you. Wear red."

"What? Why?" But Delores was gone.

Alma lifted the dish of cakes from the floor. Wear red? There had been talk at the convent about whether to continue to wear the habit. Wear red? But they were afraid they'd be just like everyone else walking the hospital halls, no differentiation, and therefore no free access either. Wear red? And be conspicuous? Without humility, all will be lost. *Yes, Saint Teresa, you are right—without humility* . . . A name? A name on a brown piece of paper. Why brown? Like wrapping paper? For mailing something? Crazy. She had plenty of white paper. Maybe some student wrote on brown and she could tear a corner off.

Alma reached over her desk to the pile of paper on the windowsill. Time to move this stuff back to her desk anyway. The door opened and Delores walked in.

"I was halfway to the elevator and I remembered some words that my uncle and cousin used to say. You can use them. Why did you get me into this anyway? Brings up too many memories—anyway, it's *Yoruba*. You could say this at the river, '*Illa mi ile oro illa mi ile oro vira ye yeye oyo ya mala.*' I think that's how it goes. Here, I'll write it down. Hand me those yellow stick-ons."

Alma handed her the stick-ons.

"Here, repeat it after me. '*Illa mi ile oro.*'"

"*Illa mi ile oro.*"

"*Vira ye yeye oyo.*"

"*Vira ye yeye oyo.*"

"*Ya mala.*"

"*Ya mala.*"

"Takes me back to when we would visit my mother's relatives in Guayama. They had this huge wraparound porch, high up off the ground. We used to play underneath with the goat and the chickens, and hide and seek, I remember. I know there's a lot more to that ritual, but you don't need it all, you just need a flavor."

"It's not like saying only half or a piece of the Apostles' Creed, is it? Like, 'I believe in the holy ghost, the holy catholic church, the communion of saints, the forgiveness of . . . and then stopping?"

"I don't know. I don't even know what it means. The creed, you know what it means, and so I guess it makes a difference. And Oshun is very forgiving anyway. My kid is going to be really mad at me if I don't get going. Bye. Wait a minute . . . I remember Oshun's color is white—no, that's Obatala's. It's . . . um . . . it's red. So wear red. See you."

"Wear red. And finish . . . forgiveness of sins, the resurrection of the body, and the life everlasting. Amen. May the Lord bless you and keep you and make his face to shine upon you for now and for evermore, quoth the raven."

Now, where's a homework on brown paper? Juan sometimes writes on a grocery bag. No, here's a lunch bag.

She tore a piece off. "I write this in remembrance of you," and she printed in large clear letters the name of the young man who had sprawled across her desk—over, under, wherever, his shirt open. "And I place your name under these honey and cinnamon cakes in the name of the Lord Jesus . . . Oshun . . . Christ . . . whomever. Amen."

May the Lord bless you and keep you, Carmelo, all the days of your young life.

Chapter 94

Carmelo is packing.

He is also crying.

"What are you blubbering about?"

"I's going."

"This your decision, bro. After you write that history of love and you get an *A*, you tell me you gonna give it up and go back? Don't be tellin' Mami I kick you out. Cut the crap, Maria. He no deserve for you to cry for him. *Mi hermano*, we gives you all we got, *pero* you wanna be a *Boriqua?* You be a *Boriqua.*"

"Shit, Mario."

"Okay, so youse did learn the English. You get *las parabalas buen*, all right—all them correct word like 'fucking' and 'shit'— and what else, *hermano, estúpido?* You got them school word too? No! You no got them words what'll get you outta Borinqueno. I guess you no wanna be rich."

"Shit, shit, shit, Mario"

"Mario, don't make him mad!"

"Shut up, Maria. Carmelo *es hermano mio.* No you brother, so shut up—and shut up the cryin' too."

Chapter 95

"Is that the move you want to make, Alma?" Father William stared across the checkerboard, took off his glasses, put them in his pocket, and pulled out his handkerchief. "I don't think you are concentrating. You have just placed yourself in the jaws of my crowned kings. Would you like to rescind that move? You can return to your previous position if you like. I will allow that."

The bishop is coming. He will ask you a question. What will your question be, Alma? Can you guess? You have to know everything if you hope to get right the one question he will ask you. Do you know your catechism? He will ask one question.

"No, thank you. I moved it there. I'll leave it there."

"You do know the consequences then," and he sprang a crowned king over the lone checker and swept if off the board.

"It's not my last piece, Father William."

"True, but what chance do you have now with only two pawns left?"

"I still have the bishop."

He will ask you one question.

Chapter 96

"Rudolfo say, when I tell him you is going back to PR, he give you money for sompin' and he ain't seen that sompin' what you was s'pose to get with the money. Is you tellin' me you done stole the money from *mi amigo*, you motherfucker?"

He should tell Mario, try to tell him… again.

"*¡Digame!* Answer me!"

"I no steal. Fuck Rudolfo. Fuck you!"

"You fuckin you bro? Here—"

"Mario, no!"

"You shut up, Maria! This between me bro and me. And 'cause you don't come clean with me or my friend, it be good you be goin' back to Mami. I still got you ticket, you know. Anoder thing, the English you is learnin' ain't no job English, like I say before. It swearing English. You stop cryin', Maria, or you is gonna get it like Carmelo." Mario turned toward Maria and pointed his fist at her.

"Mario, no! You no put no *mano* on Maria!"

His brother is not going to hit his beautiful Maria, is he? He grabbed Mario's raised arm, turned it, and with his arm underneath it, wrapped it around Mario's neck. And he should tell him. Tell him while he's got him like this. Tell him! Tell him!

"Aaaaaag Aaaag, lemme—" Mario squirmed and Maria yelled.

How can he tell him? What should he tell him? He's guilty too. Now! "Mario, *escucha! Sí, yo tango pesos, pero*—"

"Aaaaag!" Mario put his other arm over this arm lock, and they struggled until both went down, with Carmelo on top and Maria screaming, "Let go of him, Carmelo! *¡Pero*, Mario, *escucha a Carmelo!*"

"No! I ain't listenin' to nothing." Mario got loose and stood up. "*Adiós, hermano.*"

"*Tambien.* Rudolfo, he be traffacaner. He be *malo.*"

"Okay. I know he dealin' some, but that ain't you business."

"*Sí, sí.* He teach . . . he make me. You say not my *problema, pero*—"

"You mean you tellin' me he recruit? Is that what you tellin' me? You tellin me you buy for him?"

"*Sí, sí.* He say buy *para* he. He give money a me."

"I call and I check."

"No, Mario! He . . . he no call . . . he—"

"I call!"

***

"You call, Mario, *mi amigo?* I come *pronto* when you call. Here I is."

"Rudolfo! You fuckin' wid me bro?"

"Huh? Me? No."

"He say you give money so he buy."

"No, no! He need job, Mario, so he pay you rent."

"Not a drug job, Rudolfo. I tell you when he come, *escuela, pero*—"

"Yeah, you say no partner in jeans, but you no say not—"

"Shut up, *amigo*—'ceptin' you ain't no *amigo.* You fuckin' with me *hermano* here, and I no go for dat, so go. *Go!*"

234

"Geez, man, you *hermano* here is lyin', and you is buyin' his lyin', and—"

"Show him da money, bro. See dat? He no get dat from me and he no get it from no job. He get it from you to buy, and so you get out. *Get out!*"

"Geez, *amigo.*"

"See dis?"

Carmelo saw his brother's puffed-up fist, and watched Rudolfo back himself toward the door and go through it, all the time yelling, "Geez, man. Geez, man. Ya can't even stand a little—"

The door opened and a foot made Rudolfo go through it. And then it banged shut.

Chapter 97

Alma's shoes clicked. She walked quickly, not wanting anyone to stop her and ask questions, ask her about the tin tucked under her arm like a babe in bunting that would not fit in her briefcase. And how she was ever going to get to a river, she had no idea—across highways, through projects, dumps, old cars. Maybe the rain water in the curb would do.

Blessed be those who . . . the temple of the spirit is raised. "I'm on my way, Saint Anthony Mary, to find water for my little cinnamon *ebbó*, and my suffering will please you."

"Teacher, Teacher, you rush. You no rush. I did . . . I do . . . I have assignment—static electric, 'member? 'Member?"

"Mercedes? Hello, Mercedes. I . . . do rush, yes."

Alma felt a grip on her arm.

"Come, come. I have."

Alma felt a push on her back. Into a classroom. Onto a chair. Behind a desk. *Did I upset you, Saint Mary Anthony?*

"Teacher, I made research."

Made research? "Do, Mercedes, 'do research.'" Water. A river.

"Do. I do. Teacher, what that smell? Smell like—"

"Yes, well, Mercedes, research on what? On what? You use the verb 'do' with homework, research. You *make* a bed, but you *do* research. It's idiomatic, no rule, just idiomatic."

"I do it research. It cinnamon. Why you have cinnamon smell?"

236

"You *did* research. It's past. In the past. Over. Done."

"I did it research about— Why you have . . . ?"

"You *did* research. You don't need a pronoun when you already have its noun." Maybe she could just throw her *ebbó* away. No, that would be like . . . like throwing away the host? No. Not the same, not even an analogy.

"*Sí.* I write. I write you call . . . extra—"

"Yes, extra credit." How would she do that anyway, in front of Mercedes?

"*Es* about electric static."

"Wonderful."

Clink.

"What that, Teacher, on the floor? You *ebbó* tin? You have the *ebbó*?"

"I don't know what you are talking about, Mercedes. It's static electricity, not . . ." She looked at where Mercedes was pointing. Did it fall out of its bunting? The cover had come off. Exposed.

". . . electric static. The adjective comes . . ."

She reached down, pushed the lid into place, and put her foot on top. She did not look at Mercedes. Nor did she look down—which if she did she would be establishing the *ebbó* as hers.

"This is not mine. I don't know where it came from," she said, still not looking down, but keeping her foot planted on the tin. "It must have . . . I am not what you think I am. I am not a witch."

"*Yo sé.* I know. *Santeria es buena, Professora, pero en class, el papel es malo, muy malo.*"

"But you said you did research. So you can see that what happened was static electricity, right? Not voodoo. Let me see your paper."

"*Es una* Catholic? Nun. Yes, nun. A *santera y una* Catholica? *Es muy* possible."

"No. I am an Episcopalian."

"*¿Qué es? ¿Una protestante?*"

"Yes. I'm a protestant. That's all. Nothing else. Static electricity, the paper incident. It's a scientific phenomenon. You did some research, you say. So you know. Let me see the paper that you wrote—the composition, the research."

Mercedes handed Alma the paper and continued to stare and say under her breath, "*Malo y buena, malo y buena,*" while Alma read, careful to keep her foot firmly on the tin.

"The electricity of stationary charges produced by roobbing together unlike bodies, such as glass and silk, in which case equal and opposite charges are always produced . . ."

"Mercedes, I think you copied, except you misspelled 'rubbing'."

"You give *A*, Teacher? And, Teacher, you want I take *ebbó* to river?"

Alma put her head down on the desk and said softly into her arm, "No, thank you, Mercedes. I can't leave a rite unfinished."

"*¿Qué? Pero*, Teacher, you say wrong spell?"

"Yes. You wrote 'roobing.' It's 'rubbing.'"

"*¿Qué es?*"

"This." Alma reached her hand toward Mercedes, then changed its direction so that it rested on her own arm, then rubbed.

"*¿Cómo?*"

Mercedes rubbed her arm from her elbow to her wrist with vehemence, thought Alma, with a passion, as she closed both arms with both hands and said "*Cómo*" again, and Alma said, "*Sí, cómo,*" and began to rub with the other hand on the other arm also. She also crossed herself, and Mercedes looked at her and said, "Maybe, *cómo*, we do. We make that electric static—static electric."

Alma smiled. "Yes, maybe we do, but it usually happens when—"

"Teacher, you sure you no want I take *su ebbo a la river para you?*"

"Thank you, Mercedes. That's okay. I'll take care of it. Thank you anyway. I need to do this myself."

"*Comprendo, comprendo,*" Mercedes said, picking up her paper. "*Gracias por* the *A,* Teacher," She leaned down, kissed Alma on the cheek, and left the room.

Man, blinded and bowed, sits in darkness and cannot see the light of . . .

Chapter 98

The door slammed. He could hear Maria crying in the back seat of the car. The car shot forward, but Maria's crying stayed in his ears. He picked up his luggage that Mario had thrown out of the car with his last words, "You let my *amigo* fuck with you. You no stop him, *estúpido hermano.*"

Tears ran down his cheeks. He picked the luggage up that was lying on its side, half hanging off the curb into the street, and walked toward the airport door. It opened for him and he walked through, feeling swallowed. Right into all those extensions again with so many white faces. Again, not like *his* neighborhood—no whites there, just countrymen, and some blacks. His neighborhood? He was calling this shit country *his* neighborhood? Shit. And look at all these Puerto Ricans in the airport. Where were they all going? Back home like he was?

"*Quieres viajar en nuestra carreta?*"

He looked up and around at the Spanish, at whom it was directed to. Him? No, he didn't want a ride on their cart. "*Gracias, no. Gracias.*" They were going the wrong way, anyway. They were coming, heading for their luggage. Couldn't they see that he was heading for the security check to leave? What was the matter with them? They could see he was walking in the opposite direction from them with their cart. Paying money for a cart and a driver and laughing and wearing their Puerto Rican shining star tourist hats, when they weren't even tourists, and their stuff all hanging out of their bags and laughing and talking Spanish. They'll find out. They'll see!

Anyhow, it wasn't called extensions. What was the word? All these . . . these . . . rooms? Extensions? Extensions was better than rooms, but that wasn't the word. Departments? Compartments? Jesus, he knew a lot of English words! Areas, that was it. "Hey! *Areas*. The airport, it have *mucho* areas." A sentence, without any trouble!

Mario was wrong. He did learn job words. Maybe Mario was still out there, or maybe he drove back, just drove in a circle, back out there by the curb again, waiting for him to come out and get in his car so he could *tell* him he knew job English. Job English! Hey, he *knew* job English.

He swung around and started in the other direction. He could see the cart full of his countrymen up ahead, and he thought he might overtake it, and if he did, he would wave and say, "*Gracias, pero you puedo caminar mas rapido qué la carreta.*" And then he would say all that in English for them. "Thank you, *pero* I can run more fast . . . no, fast*er* as the cart! No, *than* the cart."

He stopped. Of course Mario had not done that—just gone in a circle. Mario was glad to see him go. Mario did not want him. Nor did he want Mario. Mario was a *chiflada* shithead, one minute loving him and the next minute hating him. Maybe if he got that garage job after school he could pay his *own* rent, live in another place, and soon Miguelina could come and be his wife.

And then . . . and then when we are rich, we can go back and our babies will play Dona Ana looking at the mountains and that big, big, wide sky.

He kept walking, hoping Mario *had* gone in a circle and was out there knowing he was coming back out, having changed his mind. And he would say, "Hey, bro, I got ya a coat," and if he wasn't out there, he'd get a cab and go to that garage man on Pike

Street and show him the sparka plug. No. The *spark* plug, his *A* paper, and the garage man would see it as his diploma and say, "Hey, kid, you wanna job?"

On his way, he passed the cart again, full of his countrymen on the way to *their* city of money, but they were blurry through his wet eyes.

Chapter 99

"So, did you do it yet?" Delores walked into the office. "Just curious—not that I really care."

"I started to, but I got waylaid by Mercedes's paper on static electricity. It's plagiarized."

"Don't do it if you don't want to. It's okay. I'm not invested in it, as you know."

"No, no. Honestly, I don't know how to get to the river, but I did get as far as the highway. I couldn't get across."

"There's an underpass at Seventy-Eighth Street. Go through that, walk by the marina, and just beyond the boat basin there's a break in the wall. You can get through there."

"How do you know this? You don't take *ebbós* to the river."

"We keep a boat at the marina."

"Oh. Anyhow, since I couldn't get to the river, I dropped it in a puddle instead. It probably won't work anyway. Can't I do something that doesn't involve going to a river?"

"I don't know. I suppose you could just pray, or talk to or invoke or whatever, Oshun maybe. Or I s'pose you could— You talk to saints all the time. Why don't you invoke one of your saints?"

"I don't think my . . . They are for a different purpose. I don't pray to them. I just say what they say . . . said. But I really have to finish."

"Okay, then. At least go to some water someplace and put five cents with the *ebbó*. That goes to your orisha. But darned if

I know how she or he gets it. By the way, some of your saints are probably syncretized with a Yoruba god, so you could find out which are, and then you could name—"

"This is crazy."

"I told you it was, but you're in it now, and you should really finish, like you said. If I were you, I'd just pray to Oshun and then go back to the puddle, hope the cakes are still in that puddle, and toss them in the river."

"Tossing them seems so irreverent, but I guess using a puddle was too."

"No different from dunking a kid for baptism."

"'Immerse' is the word."

"Ok. Immerse. Go immerse your cakes in the river."

Hear God's word, ye fishes of the sea and river.

Chapter 100

Alma touched the red beret that was topping her head like a lamp. She tightened the red scarf against the wind. At first she thought the tin was no longer in that puddle, but a *V* of light from a speeding car landed on something that was square and certainly not a stone. She leaned down and picked it out of the grimy water. She wiped it on her scarf, looked carefully at it, opened it, and yes, there were the cinnamon cakes, unruffled. Now she had no reason to not do this the right way.

And, yes, there was the underpass. And the river beyond. Not calm. A bit turbulent. Could wash the *ebbó* away. The white caps looked like the edging of her headpiece, with the grey water flowing madly behind. Sister Augusta always put her hood up when she went out, and her big, heavy down coat left only a few inches of habit on her forehead and down below. You couldn't hear the swoosh under all that thick coat—sort of like this traffic.

Her nun days swam in front of her and saints invaded her.

Avoid heretics like wild beasts; for they are mad dogs, biting secretly.

***

Now she could tell Delores that she had done it. Now she could finish up the self-study and make up the final exam and not worry about Carmelo anymore.

I go, Teacher. A PR, Teacher. No end class. You teacher bueno. Mi, no estudiante bueno.

Not true, Carmelo. You should stay.

No, no, no. Miguelina—

Yes, yes, I understand.

But she didn't. How could he love so many?

The soul cannot live without love. All depends on providing it with a worthy subject.

Chapter 101

"You have mail, Alma. It's on your desk. I picked it up for you. Actually thought it was a memo from the dean."

How could she think that? It was a postcard. She was curious. Nosy. *Can't blame her.*

"*Ola*, Teacher Alma. *Yo* . . . I have . . . has . . . have the job. I the collision man. I no has to talk English to fit a break car brake. Miguelina *es mi* wife. We marrie. I have happy. You be *contento?*"

Alma stuck both thumbs in her eyes to stop what was about to become a throbbing flood.

"I read it, Alma. Forgive me. Go ahead and cry. I don't blame you."

Alma put her head on her desk and wrapped her arm around it.

The door opened. "Hi, ladies. Professor Hedman, just poking my head in to make sure you haven't hit any wrong keys. I know the dean . . . he mentioned to me . . ."

Alma lifted her head. "Sorry, didn't mean to. I just got to my office."

"As I say, the dean mentioned at the last chair's meeting that he would have the report by . . . Anyway, thought I'd pass that along."

"Yes, he'll have it."

We have only one evil to fear, and that is sin.

"Tomorrow. After Klinghoffen's class . . . about . . . apostolic, I mean . . . ordering, cyclic rule ordering."

"Good. I'll let him know."

Chapter 102

Alma leafed through her notebook. Professor Klinghoffen scratched the board with a piece of chalk. Alma scratched her pen on the paper in her notebook. *Cyclic rule ordering . . . here . . . pieces of notes.* Why couldn't she finish sentences? Why didn't she transcribe these bits into intelligible wholes? *Mother was right. Nothing gets finished.*

She'd better stop this and listen to this professor.

"On reflexive transformation . . . well, yes, read Lees and Klima's *Rules for English Pronominalization.*" Professor Klinghoffen rummaged in his briefcase. "Don't seem to have it with me. At any rate, read that, and we'll move onto the null concept. Remember, a sentence is never ambiguous in context. If it is, one must disambiguate by adding another sentence to clarify. Meaning is at least choice."

Yes, that was true, but she was becoming very sleepy, and her self-study was sliding around in her head. She felt her eyelids move down.

"Meaning is at least choice, as I said, para-medic contrast— boy/girl . . ."

Yes, go on Professor.

". . . syntagmatic contradicts, collocational features— identified with Chomsky features . . ."

I'm listening, Professor, honest.

". . . we base generate the derived nominals. Do not for gerundive nominals—that happens by affix-hopping . . ."

Just a catnap for a second, won't miss much.

Alma's chin dropped into the palm of her hand. *And affix-hopping onto Nurys's half-naked body blatant . . .*

". . . cyclic rule applies to passive. A system without a subject doesn't meet quality control . . ."

Like a right breast, clean-shaven . . .

"Chomsky explained, idioms are strong collocations . . . necessarily mean you can come up with semantic interpretation . . ."

The shaver would do a better, a cleaner job . . .

"Certain combinations are idioms, and thus entered as lexicon items, but some aren't, like 'lost his cool' . . ."

He certainly did, on her desk, like that—lose his cool. And whatever happened to the null concept? Isn't that what this lecture, and the last, was all about? Who got lost, she or Professor Klinghoffen?

"Just a general review, class, of the null hypothesis, but before I do that, let me remind you that your papers are due Monday."

Papers? How about a self-study? It's full of null concepts!

Chapter 103

Memo

To: Professor Alma Headman

It appears that the self-study report, which you have submitted, is flawed. I do notice that affixed to the cover letter is a note to the effect that this is draft number one. You do realize, don't you, that we have a deadline?

On another note, I can only assume that your second, and hopefully final, draft will be, shall we say, Carmelo free. I noted one or two references to, I assume, a student, and do not believe such references need to be included in this Reaccreditation Report for Middle States.

The facts speak for themselves in this type of report.

I look forward to the final draft.

Dean

Raise up your heart after a fall. Do not be astonished at your weakness.

Chapter 104

Rudolfo parked his truck. He got out. "C'mon, Ceil, let's go find her. We sign her, she'll be on our team. You talk when we meet her, greet her, right, Ceil?"

"Yeah, but this here too near the school, and it got no good memories for me, with you all in a fight and stuff. And that crazy—what's his name, Carmelo? Throwing our stuff on the street like he did."

"Don't worry, Ceil. That fightin' dude ain't here no more. Got chicken. Fled home to mama, where he gonna be pickin' mangos and pumpin' gas for cash. Look. See? That be her.

"Nurys! Nurys!"

Nurys turned around.

"Missin' your boyfriend?"

Nurys flipped her chin and walked on.

"That stupid to say, Rudolfo." Ceil leaned on the truck.

"No, no, Nurys. I not mean that. I want you. We want you. We hear you was good at negotiations and business and figuring and all that, and could use a job. We need . . . c'mon!"

Nurys turned back and shook her head at Rudolfo, and then turned again and walked on.

"Hey, Nurys! This here Ceil. She good. You be workin' with her, and get good money. And don't you worry, that dude you like? He be back when he get tired a lizards crawlin' on his feet. Hey, you remember me, don't you?"

But Nurys was running toward a woman and calling, "Teacher Alma! Teacher wait up on me!"

She caught up with Alma, and they both went through the door to security together, both missing something in their lives, but neither planning to say what it was.

CHAPTER 105

Memo
> To: Dean
> Accompanying this memo is the final draft of the Self-Study Report for the Reaccreditation of the college, and I assure you it is, as you say, Carmelo free. You are right, the report must not include student stories as illustrations of problems or to place emphasis on critical issues, either positive or negative. I have, therefore, made sure that every possible trace of the fictional student, Carmelo, has been deleted from this report.
>
> Thank you for giving me the opportunity to learn about and be involved in this crucial understanding of the college.

***

Alma printed out the memo and attached it to the top of the cover page of the report, clipped the individual sections together, along with the charts and appendices, in the accepted organized manner, studiously following the guidelines supplied to her, put the package into an envelope—also supplied to her—and climbed the stairs to the second floor, walked down the hall, and knocked on the dean's office door.

Alma held out her hand to the dean. The dean took it, shook it weakly, not looking at her, and said, "Thank you for telling me of your progress. I assume this is the final."

He went to his desk, sat down, and opened the folder. "Adiós," he said without looking up.

Alma left the office. She walked along the hall slowly. Her briefcase bumped against her thigh. She tried to hold her hand and arm steady so that it would not bump that way. She should have stayed at Saint Beggia's. No one asked her to reaccredit a school there.

All the ways of this world are as fickle and unstable . . .

At Saint Beggia's, her briefcase could not be felt by her thigh. It didn't bump it when she walked. If it did, she didn't feel it. And it held only student papers, not periodic review report drafts for reaccreditation by the Eastern States Association for Accreditation of Multi-lingual Special Pedagogical . . .

Bump, bump, bump . . .

Was that Professor Comen walking toward her? She should turn around before—

"I see you coming from the dean's office, Professor Hedman."

Too late to turn around.

"You must still prove yourself in other ways, besides the self-study, that is, if you want your personnel file to be adequate and complete for reappointment in the fall."

Her briefcase bumped in time with her steps. "I assume you are referring to my being enrolled in a PhD program," she said as she got closer.

"Yes, but I realize that that may be too much to ask of you. Even though, without that, your tenure is in question."

"The GREs are under my belt, and I have been accepted and have begun classes." Alma walked by her, leaving Professor Comen with her mouth open. She walked toward the elevator.

Bump, bump, bump . . .

Ignore the devil . . . He trembles and flees at your guardian angel's sight.

Chapter 106

"Certainly an old desk," Alma mumbled, "with a hole for an inkwell, ridges at the top for pens, pencils, peanuts, whatever. This university must have bought a bunch of old desks from a defunct school."

Alma looked up from the desk and watched Professor Klinghoffen write Greek letters on the blackboard. He was saying something on which she should probably be taking notes.

"The Greek alphabetical script was derived from a Semitic form of writing . . ."

She rubbed her finger in a circle around the edge of the napkin ring as it dangled around her neck.

". . . employs some letters that originally represented consonants for vowel sounds . . ."

She grabbed it as it swung from left to right across her chest and pulled it over her head. She held it over the inkwell, measured it with her eye, and dropped it in. The cross made a slight dinging sound as it traveled with the ring into the hole. The snug fit of the cross in the napkin ring caused her a small amount of excitement, but she pushed the feeling away as being not an appropriate response to snug fitting.

". . . used from the beginning of the first millennium BC for the writing of Greek. Notice the stress on the vowel when . . ."

Alma's eyelids moved down over her eyeballs.

". . . count three from the ultimo . . ."

She jerked her head up.

"... if the accent is on the last syllable ..."

Maybe if she opened her eyes wide and wider and stared at ... at ...

"... the generative and dative ..."

No, too obvious. She should move her eyelids down just a little, so as not to be so ...

"... last three syllables are the penult and ultima ..."

Oh, the angel danced on the head of a pin. Wake up, wake up! See the angel dance on the head of a pin. How many, how many could make that spin, do that spin, could spin, spin, spin? Must think about cadence, beat.

Alma opened her eyes all the way. She forced them to stay open. Must think about cadence, beat, as well as clarity. She fiddled with the napkin ring. She tried to pull it out of the inkwell hole. That activity might keep her eyelids up where they belonged. It was time to retrieve the napkin ring anyway, but since it fit so well, so neatly, it would not lift. She tucked the tip of her fingernail underneath the horizontal portion of the cross and lifted, carefully, so as not to jar the position of the cross in the ring.

"Let's move on, now, to the agglutinative character of the Kirundi verb ..."

Her fingers surrounded the cross as it also dangled from the napkin ring itself.

"Turn your attention, for the moment, please, to the agglutinative nature of the languages other than Kirundi of which there are quite a few."

The spirit longs for fruition. Now begins an eternal craving and insatiable longing..

Chapter 107

The Underlying Syntactical Structure of Negatives and Interrogatives, As Well As Other Discontinuities, is Rule-Based

Null Hypothesis: The omission of the auxiliary morpheme by the subjects to be tested is an example of fossilization and cannot be overcome after the critical period has passed.

An adequate theory of natural language must allow grammar to capture the richness of all possible languages, including Carmelo's, especially Carmelo's, and must provide rules—hear that, Carmelo?—for a fixed phonetic alphabet and for means of notation that are more than merely taxonomic.

Draft:

Paragraph I: An adequate theory must make it possible for the ideal speaker-hearer to produce and understand sentences never before uttered or heard, at least by the speaker-hearer, such as "I do." Such a theory must take into consideration complexities, ambiguities, permutations, discontinuities—*Did he show up, Miguelina? Was he there at the altar when you pirouetted with your father before following the flower girl dressed as a miniature bride, as are we all, Miguelina, brides of our*

Father in heaven? Dearly beloved, we have come together . . .—and, by taking into consideration complexities, ambiguities, permutations and discontinuities does not allow deviancy . . .

"Do you still have a good relationship with the computer?" Professor Alverez leaned over Alma's shoulder and looked at the computer screen.

She looked up. Where did he come from? Wasn't here a minute ago.

"Not clicking any wrong buttons anymore, are you?"

"I finished the report."

"Good. Without mishap?"

"Yes. It's in the dean's hands."

"So what are you doing here this late? Before you hit a wrong key again and send whatever you are doing into space, let's go for coffee."

"I have a paper due tomorrow for my lin—"

"Write it at home. You can't stay here any longer. The guards are locking up, so whatever you're doing, it's time to stop."

"I need to finish my thought. Did you know that no amount of phrase-structure rules can account for passive constructions?"

"Makes sense to me. Where's your coat?"

"And no amount of phrase-structure rules can account for—"

"You said that. By the way, what's this around your neck? I noticed it last week and was curious."

"You're interrupting me again, and I had such a beautiful conclusion in mind."

"You'll remember it."

"No, it's gone." Alma slumped into her chair, letting her gathered papers fall.

"For Christ's sake, Alma." Professor Alverez leaned down and began picking the papers up off the floor.

Alma looked at the shoulder that was next to her knee, at the back, so smooth.

"You could help, too, you know. These *are* your papers."

She put her hand on the shoulder, and then moved it onto the back, leaning toward the shoulder as she did this. She continued to lean, an adequate theory of natural language, and reached her right hand down toward her scattered papers, leaving the other hand on the shoulder.

"I remember what my conclusion was," she said, and moved her hand off the shoulder and down toward the papers on the floor.

"Good. Keep picking up papers, please."

"Something about single phrase-markers and making involved rules to allow for conjunctions and then—"

"Don't stop."

"I'm not. And then trying to capture the co-occurrence relationship. But I'm not sure what all this has to do with my null hypothesis, and—or my title."

"What's your title? Come on, just a few more."

"The Missing Is."

"Right. There's a paper over there."

"I'll get it."

I wrote a name on a brown piece of paper. Carmelo. I took it to the river and baptized it. It floated away. I saw it go.

"That's a pretty good conclusion I came up with, don't you think?"

"Do you mean trying to capture the co-occurrence relationship? Not a bad title either."

"That and . . ." *A name on a piece of paper.*

"What are you whispering now? Sweet nothings? You can do that over coffee. Now, put these papers in some sort of order and let's go. Aaaaand answer my question."

"What question?"

"What's that around your neck?"

"My napkin ring from the convent."

"And the cross in it? I guess that means . . . what?"

"I don't know. I just like—"

"That you're married to God?"

"I just remembered part of my conclusion: 'An adequate theory of natural language has to be operative for all strings of all languages, and on all levels, morphological, phonological, and syntactical.'"

"I suppose you are going to quote saints to me next. I heard one of your students say that you did that in class—that you talk at yourself like you are talking to saints."

"I . . . I . . ."

"It's okay. Let's go. By the way, you can be married to God and still be married in life too, you know."

Alma reached for her coat. She fiddled with the napkin ring. She had not thought about the meaning when she stuck the cross in. Only that it fit so well, and that they went together so well.

"Did you hear what I said, Alma?"

"Yes, and see how well these fit together?" She held the napkin ring away from her chest, and Professor Alverez picked it up and cradled it in his hand.

"Yes, it does fit snugly. Can you take it off and let me see it more closely?"

"I guess." Alma unclipped the back. It slid from her neck and fell onto her desk.

Clunk!

Chapter 108

Dear Alma,

    When I tell the aunts that I don't hear from you very much, if ever, they say, "Oh dear, oh dear."

Endlogue

"I understand that the *Hallelujah Chorus* is joyous, but to bounce in your chair like a clown, Alma, is not appropriate to do in church."

"No one can live without joy."

"I'm not arguing against joy, dear, and I'm familiar with Thomas's statement, but perhaps you need to finish his thought."

"And that is why a man deprived of spiritual joy goes over to carnal pleasures?"

"Exactly."

"It is always springtime in the heart that loves God."

"I am also familiar with the wisdom of the saints, Alma. And we are in a church, so—"

"Be merry, really merry. The life of a true Christian—"

"Alma, add to your nightly prayers one that says, 'Help me, God, to not feel the necessity to have the last word.'"

GLOSSARY

CHAPTER 4

Mi equipaje: My luggage
Pero por qué tu me hablas en Inglés siempre?: But why do you speak to me in English?
Primero el trabajo: First work
Comprendo, si—tambien—el trabajo. La escuela es para menores: I understand, yes—also—work. School is for children.
Ahora: Now
Qué: What
Quién es: Who is
Vete a la escuela: Go to school

CHAPTER 6

Escucha: Listen
Mira: Look (see)
El trabajo ahora: Work now
Otra: other
Plantons: bananas
Dónde?: where
Es papi's: It's Papa's

CHAPTER 10

Entonces: Then/so
"Recuerde Guayabo": Remember Guayabo
Muchachito: Young boy
Mano: Hand
Escuela: school
Pavo: turkey

CHAPTER 12

Sí sí: Yes
No sé: I don't know
Pero: But
Tu loco: You're crazy
Qué es: What is
Gracias: Thanks
De nada: You're welcome (it's nothing)
Habla Español: Do you speak Spanish
Dónde: Where
Un pequito: A little
Aquí: Here
Ahora: Now
Vette (off) con mío: Get off with me
…Buena para tu: It'll be good for you
Bueno bueno. Sé algunas palabras una palabra por otra, una palabra aquí y allá…": Good good. There be some words, one for another, a word here and there
No llores: Don't cry…(I shouldn't cry)
Malo: Bad
"Toma … hijo de la gran puta—maricon me cago en tu madre, toma,": "Take that…son of a bitch—I shit on your mother, take that,"
"¡Muchachito cogelo suavesito!…": "Take it easy, kid"

266

CHAPTER 14

"Por qué yo no trabajo?: "Why don't I find work"
Trabajos y munera: Work and money
Pavo estúpido: stupid turkey
Pero con todo: But for all that

CHAPTER 16

tío: uncle
"Las Puertoriquenas son unas iguarantes y putas: Puerto Ricans are ignorant whores
Bueno: Good
A si llamas!: Oh yes, name

CHAPTER 17

Aquí… haz cola conmigo. Puedes meterte delante mi. Ves aquel hombre alla? Es el scanner. Sabes, para armas y cosas… cuchillos.": Here…wait with me. You can get in front of me. You see that man there? He is the scanner. You know—for weapons and knives.
Tu… vente!": You come
Cómo sé llama?: What is your name?
El Moro and El Queda: Fortresses
Muy simpatico: Very nice
Es de la baja: This is to go down
Vente de la arriba: This is to go up

CHAPTER 20

Estudiante Nuevo: New student
Quiero classe en: I want a class in

Un pequito: A little bit
Sientese: Sit down
Tu loco: You're crazy

CHAPTER 22

"Ninguna ha mi documentos?": Don't have my documents (does anyone see my documents?)
"Ay alguin qué tienes mis documentos?": Does anyone have (or seen) my documents?
Dios míos: My God
Por qué: Why

CHAPTER 23

"Es uno brujo qué no puedo…": It's a witch who cannot… (decide whether to come in or not)
"Loco…violenta…enfadado.": Crazy…violent…angry (mad)
Otra …es bueno: Other…this is good
Muy bonita: Very pretty
Silencio por favor: Please be quiet
"Por qué estas en la clase de Inglés: Why are you in this English class?
En clase mismo?: Are we in the same class?
Ayer: yesterday
Semana…dos, tres semana…pasada: A week …two, three weeks…ago

CHAPTER 25

Pero, entendez: But, understand
No quero trabajo con ese: I do not want to work with that

Dice en Español: Talk in Spanish
Es mi amor: (she) is my love
Besame: Kiss me
muy bonita: very pretty
Yo no sé: I don't know

CHAPTER 31

Oiteh: Listen to yourself. (Did you hear what you just said)
Pero no trabajo: But not work...

CHAPTER 34

"Duermete Mi Niño": "Sleep my child"
dice returno: He says he will return
Quién sabe: Who do you know?
El dice el tío: (She will) talk to his uncle
Lunes: Monday

CHAPTER 35

Loco niño: Crazy kid
No quiere: (She) doesn't want

CHAPTER 37

Yo vengo a la escuela: I go to school
Vete a la escuela: Go to school
Hermano de sangre: Blood brother

CHAPTER 38

Aquí. Aquí el garage. Entro... saludo al jefe. Hablo Inglés...
aprendo... digo 'Vengo despues de escuela...y trabajo' pero en

Inglés: Here. Here is a garage. I enter (First I go in)…say hello to the boss. I talk in English…I learn it. (I tell him I'm learning it)….I say 'I come after school…and work' but in English (but I say it in English)
Pregunta: Ask
Pero quién: But who
Olvidé decirle no eat ése barra de caramelo: I forgot to tell him not to eat the candy bar
Dios mío: My God

CHAPTER 40

"Yo tengo…..por su tío": I have….for your uncle
….Yo tengo para amigo de mi hermano—pero no es mi amigo, pero: … I have for your brother's friend—but he is not my friend, but

CHAPTER 43

despojos: cleansings
ebbós: protective spells

CHAPTER 45

digame: tell me

CHAPTER 46

Ella es bruja: She is a witch
Blanca….cómo luna: White …like (the) moon
Toma: Take one

CHAPTER 49

Todos los classe escribe en: The whole class writes in
Mañana: tomorrow

CHAPTER 50

Abuelo: grandfather
"Medias lunas de oro y de el mármol verde jade y un hombre vendiendo naranjas peladas…": Half moons of gold and marble green jade and a man selling peeled oranges
Miro…pequeño…blanco con cabeza y cascabel pequeño la piel sintetica.: See… a small… white head with small synthetic bells (rattle)
Yo trato: I try
No sabe: I don't know

CHAPTER 51

Tonto: Idiot
Ojalateria: A mechanic (tin man)
Y no malo hasta la médula cómo: And not bad to the core like
El coquí: A kind of a lizard that has special meaning in Puerto Rico
casa: house

CHAPTER 53

chiflada: crazy
orisha: god or goddess (Yoruba)
Para la puerta: By the door
Oyes: You hear?

Tango moola: I have the money
Oyes: Look at him like that
Habla chico: Speak boy
Me olvido: I forget

CHAPTER 56

Disculpar: I apologize (forgive me)
Es muy dificil dar explicaciones o de entender: It is very difficult to explain or to understand
...esé yo excribo. Pero no escribo esé. Yo escribo ...: ...that I write. But I don't write that. I write...
Pero ...vente y ....Closo me mate...: But... he'll come and... kill me
Dice a mí: (Rudolfo) tell me that

CHAPTER 58

...I no puedo pregunto por mas: ...I can't ask for more
Pero es tarde: But it is late
Es deficil: It's difficult
Pero yo sabe ese (game).......Pero ...jamás sabe con ese (ending): But I know that...But...never did I know that
No sabe: Don't know

CHAPTER 61

Curandero: Healer

CHAPTER 62

Oshún: Goddess of love
Illa mi ile oro illa mi ile oro vira ye yeye oyo vira ye yeye oro: Magic chant

Ya mala ya mala: Already bad already bad
Jamás: never

CHAPTER 63

...qué hacer en mi escuela?: ...what are you doing in my school?
No confias en me?: You don't have confidence in me?
"Quieres conocer a mi professora?": "You want to know my professor?"
nada nada: nothing nothing
mi oyes, mi hermano: You, Bro, you listen to me
Ella no sé una palabra (English): She doesn't know a word (in English)?

CHAPTER 70

"Todos mis problemas comenzaron ese dia. Todos mis problemas han sido desde ese dia: "All my problems began that day. All my problems have been since that day

CHAPTER 72

"O (even) uno cemento en San Juan: Or a cement (house) in San Juan (small and cheap)
Todos los classe escribe en English now: Everybody in the class to everybody in the class writes in English now

CHAPTER 73

"Alumnos: Estan por cerrar nuestro colegio. Pero no lo lograran. Tenemos demasiado poder para ellow hacer eso. Pero hay dos puntos mas que son y no son ralacionados. Es sobre la proposicion del aumento de la ensenanza: "Students: They are about to close our college. But they will not do that. We have too much power for them to do that. But there are two other issues that are related but not related. One is about the proposition to raise our tuition

CHAPTER 76

A (motor) decil es mismo: A decil (motor) is the same
…pero no tiene un carburador: …but it doesn't have a carberator
papel: paper

CHAPTER 81

cuando: when
Si hay un temblequeo: If there is a shiver (shake)
Tembloroso: Trembling (shaking)
Es necesario qué el combustible sea puro: It is necessary that the fuel be pure
…hijo de la gran puta—maricon…y tu madre: …son of a bitch—faggot … and your mother
"cremo y leche de la Evaristo y Peche": "cream and milk of Evaristo and Peche"

CHAPTER 83

bambino: little one
nombre: name
Dega me salir el de este armario: I'll get out of this closet

CHAPTER 94

Boriqua: A poor area

CHAPTER 98

"Quieres viajar en nuestra carreta?: "Do you want a ride on our cart?"

Review Requested:

If you loved this book, would you please provide
a review at Amazon.com?